BLUE STAR

THE TERRAROMA TRILOGY PART TWO

DAVID ROSS FINDLAY

FriesenPress

One Printers Way
Altona, MB R0G 0B0
Canada

www.friesenpress.com

Copyright © 2022 by David Ross Findlay
First Edition — 2022

All rights reserved.

No part of this publication may be reproduced in any form, or by any means, electronic or mechanical, including photocopying, recording, or any information browsing, storage, or retrieval system, without permission in writing from FriesenPress.

Illustrated by Keith Jenkinson

ISBN
w978-1-03-911228-5 (Hardcover)
978-1-03-911227-8 (Paperback)
978-1-03-911229-2 (eBook)

1. FICTION, SCIENCE FICTION, ADVENTURE

Distributed to the trade by The Ingram Book Company

TERRAROMA

1

THE GREAT UNKNOWN

NO ONE COMES out here, Brent thought as he imagined their ship sinking deeper into the darkness. *No one ever takes a course like this, anyway. Why would they? It was practically like burning money.* The spaceship he was aboard, a small trader-class ship, was indeed on a strange course. A course that was designed to avoid detection, which was his stock and trade. He was, for lack of a better name, a smuggler.

The ship, *The Maryjane,* had passed through the Martian trade routes and had now arched high over the ellipsis of the solar system. Maybe tomorrow, when he felt they had cleared enough of the asteroid belt, he could punch the engine and make some good time.

There were two other people in his crew: Simon, who was now passed out drunk after securing the cargo for the high-speed travel ahead, and Helen, who was in the aft, working on communication concerns that would no doubt come up soon enough. Permits for fake cargo, travel and flight plans, and most importantly the new credentials that Brent had as captain. Those credentials had never been tested, and he hated going out on a job with unsecured credentials. There was a joke in there somewhere, and he supposed that he'd get the punchline on the day the cell door slammed shut.

Brent sat on the bridge with his view screen split between three angles: forward, aft, and below. No real reason for the screens; the idea that he could watch for trouble was ridiculous, and he knew the parameters he had set for the sensors would catch something before his eyes ever would. But it made him feel better, and he was far more nervous this time out than he usually was.

He had good reasons for his case of the nerves, two of them. First, this was planned to be his last job, and the payoff was big, big enough to keep him on the straight and narrow for the rest of his life. This one had to work out, and then he was set. Second was the cargo that they were carrying and the people they were delivering it to. The buyers were considered to be terrorists by the solar system government, although Brent personally felt that they were stretching the definition of the label. The buyers were homesteaders on the moon of Iapetus, with rather unique political views. "Homesteaders" was Brents euphemism, so he didn't have to consider the fact that he was doing business with terrorists. They needed some negotiating chips to find their place in the solar system. The cargo that Brent was delivering was two 50-megaton warheads.

Over the course of time, he had moved a great deal of all kinds of contraband all over the system. Some months, back he had come to the conclusion that he was tired of doing small jobs and risking his licence; he wanted a way out. One final big job could do the trick, and he could retire from the smuggling and operate as a legal trader. That was the plan, anyway.

So, Brent was having a hard time relaxing today. To look at him, John Brent could have been a diplomat or a law officer; short-cropped blond hair, well-groomed, and dressed in fairly stylish clothes of the time. Six feet tall, in good physical shape for his fifty-five years, which was still pretty youthful for the times. He always did his best to not look like a smuggler. He no longer really wished to be a smuggler, and he hoped this job would pay well enough for him to get out of the business.

The panel in front of Brent beeped, and he looked down at it.

"Shit," he croaked and cleared his throat. "Bealzabub, give me something on that blip and make sure our screens are up. I don't want us getting scanned." He was addressing the ship's AI system, a second-grade assistant he had modified to have a bit more personality than the standard flat drone.

"Jeepers, it's the cops, Dude! Actually, it's a peacekeeper patrol ship." The AI spoke aloud and Brent winced. "It's about to hail us."

The panel let out a squeak that served as the hail.

"Send them our codes, Bub," Brent told the computer.

Long moments went by, and Brent watched the peacekeeper patrol ship grow rapidly in size on the aft viewer. Finally, the hail sounded again, and this time, Brent knew that he had to answer in person. He punched a button on the consul and spoke.

"Trader D910091, we're doing fine here, thanks, folks. Over."

"Please repeat your codes and drop your screens, trader. Over," said a serious female voice.

Now I'm in it, Brent thought. This was what he had feared; that they would encounter some hard-assed patrol that wouldn't accept his codes at face value. If he dropped the screens, they would likely insist on boarding the trader, and he couldn't allow that to happen. They were doing more than a standard patrol; they were looking for something. He typed a message to Helen and hoped that she already knew what was going on; her job had been to make sure there was no stray info in the ship's computer drives that could trip them up. He didn't drop the screens yet. He was thinking as fast as he could, but it seemed his options were limited.

They were fucked. He knew it. Now he stopped fooling himself and went into action. Drastic measures. Survival mode. He clicked the panel and, this time, spoke throughout the trader.

"Strap in. This is it! Helen, is that asshole strapped down?"

"I secured him as soon as he passed out." Helen's voice came back through the console.

"Good work! Strap yourself in. I'm gonna punch it and see what these new boosters can do."

"Don't wait for me!"

"Peacekeeper, we're happy to cooperate any way we can," Brent said into the panel. "No need to be unfriendly"

"Trader, drop your screens now. If you do not comply ..."

Brent hit it. The little trader ship accelerated so fast that the peacekeeper's grappler, which advanced without warning, caught nothing but empty space. Not giving them a moment to react, Brent hit both the slip engines *and* the boosters again, and they were gone at an advanced speed, the course already programmed into Bealzabub. He couldn't really relax yet, but it looked like the trick had worked for the moment. The small trader continued to gain speed at an exponential rate until they were far, far away from where they had encountered the peacekeeper.

He shut the boosters off, then released the clamp that kept him safely locked into his seat. He stood up and his boots magnetized. He walked to the back of the bridge in a somewhat clunky fashion. It always took a while to get the rhythm of walking in magnetized boots, no matter how many times you did it. He could hear the locks opening as Helen travelled through the ship to the bridge.

The door opened, and Helen appeared. She was a tall, slim-framed woman, a beautiful mix of European and Asian genes. Helen was fifty-one years old and a veteran of space travel. She had been all over the solar system. She was generally reserved but friendly enough. She understood the risks and the rewards of the actions they were taking. Brent had no idea how she got into the smuggling game, but she came highly recommended. She stepped into the room, and although her movements were dictated by her magnetized boots, she managed to move more elegantly than Brent.

"We've got to get the hell out of here," she said. "They're gonna be looking for us for sure."

"Am I correct in assuming that you'll know if they find us?" Brent said. He knew that Helen Furtado had software in her head that was called, among other things, a Dark Monitor. She could detect subspace radio transmissions and probing sensors *in her head*. To have some type of brain augmentation or *wetware* was as common in their century as carrying a cellphone had been in the twenty-first century. Helen, however, had special software that was highly illegal. It gave them a great advantage in avoiding the authorities.

"Yes," she replied. "But it's not 100 percent, as you saw. They were running silent when they came up on us. That peacekeeper is looking for something." She moved across the bridge to one of the two seats that sat before the compact console. "You should change our heading," She worked at the board. "And hit the boosters again."

"Those boosters are expensive," he said as he took the other chair.

"After the deal is done, you can buy all the boosters you want," Helen said impassively with a sideways glance.

Helen had a quiet severity about her, and Brent liked that very much. He gave a small sigh and promised himself to be professional. Helen's reputation in the business of moving illegal goods was second to none; she was also well known to take zero bullshit from admiring team members. That was fine with Brent; they were here to make money, not party.

Brent hit the boosters again, as she had suggested, and the ship lurched forward for several seconds as they both hung onto grapples on the bridge bulkheads.

From below, Simon was hailing the bridge. Brent assumed that he would be miserable and hungover.

"What the hell is going on out there?" came his Afrikaans/Martian accent. "I almost puked on myself, waking up accelling at that g." His voice crackled a bit and went dead with an inaudible curse. Simon was on his way up.

"Oh my God," Helen said in a tone of voice that Brent had never heard from her before. She sat at the controls, occasionally looking down at the board, and then staring into space. He assumed she was using that special software in her head.

"Don't tell me that they've found us that fast?" Brent groaned. A moment later, Simon walked onto the bridge. He was tall, thin, and dark; like many who have grown up in a lighter g, he looked spindly and had a tendency to stoop.

"Bloody hell!" said the newcomer.

Helen frowned. "No, I don't mean that. There's nothing out there."

"Okay, then that's good. We're in the clear then," Brent said nervously, his gut telling him it wouldn't be that simple. He was right.

"I mean that there's nothing out there at all! *The goddamn stars are gone—where the fuck are the stars?*" Helen exclaimed, her voice straining.

"Aw, come on. It's gotta be a glitch, sensor failure," Simon put forward.

"No. No, it's not," Helen said. "There's nothing wrong with my head and it's like an echo chamber out there, with nothing to make a sound. The emptiness is horrible. Where are we?"

They all went over the controls and sensor readings. They came to the agreement that there was no equipment failure that they could understand. They seemed to be accelerating into nothing. They couldn't get a course heading that made any sense to them.

Finally, Brent put the ship's AI on the task of explaining what had happened to them. Helen sat still in her chair, quietly awaiting an explanation. Simon paced the bridge in a clunky manner for a short time and finally shut off his boots and hung in the air.

Shortly, the AI spoke up through the main console. "Well, Boss, the truth is we are nowhere. Our last known position in space was 20 AU above solar plane, over Jupiter. It had to be somewhere near there that we passed into *this region of space*. We are in a void outside of normal space. This space is much emptier than normal space. There are fewer molecules per cubic metre than in normal space, and I can achieve no bearings in normal space/time. Please note that the chronometers are behaving strangely, and the last true readings are inconclusive. There are no points of reference in this void."

"That peacekeeper would have been doing their best to track us," Helen said. "The last echo reflect in my wetware tells me that they were closer behind us than we realized—sneaking up on us, if you can believe that—and then they were gone, or we were gone. I've never seen anything like this before, and I've seen some strange readings in deep space."

No one spoke for a moment. They all just stood around, lost in their own private thoughts. There was no sound at all but the occasional hum of the engines, a sound that only served to remind Brent of the facts that he could not reconcile. *We're still accelerating into what?* This was his job, and he felt that he should reach for some explanation, even if he wasn't buying it himself. Finally, he spoke.

"Okay, let's not get ahead of ourselves, people. We've probably entered into a magnetic cloud, and it's playing hell with our instruments. Let's just keep going, and we're bound to clear it in a while." No one made a response just then. These were two of the toughest people in the game, and Brent knew they didn't spook easily. He doubted they were buying into the magnetic cloud theory, but this was his mission, and he felt like he should say something to raise morale.

"If there's nothing to do, then we do nothing," said Helen curtly. "I'm going to try and get some rest."

"Can you still monitor?" Brent asked.

"I put the Dark Monitor on standby a little while ago. The empty echo is unnerving. It'll still scan even when I'm asleep. An alarm will wake me if there's anything."

"I trust you more than I trust Bub's sensors at the moment," Brent said.

Helen didn't reply but made seconds-long eye contact for the first time since he hired her. She went below decks, leaving Brent and Simon on the bridge to contemplate the void. They took turns sitting before the console and listening to random music supplied by Bealzabub. Hours passed, and the two men hardly spoke.

Simon also was a legend in the business of moving illegal merchandise. It was said that he had once stolen a Martian racer and then sold it back to the original owner a day before the Interplanetary Space Race. Simon had to be in his sixties by the look of him, but he was probably older. It was almost impossible to tell anyone's real age anymore unless they were straight with you about it. Brent was fifty-five, which was young to be looking to retire at anything in these times. Well, first retirement anyway; people have been known to make a comeback as late as eighty. By the time a person reaches 120, they usually settle down and truly "retire." Shortly before it was time for Brent to take his sleep period, Helen called up to the bridge.

"There *is* something out there. An SOS, a beacon on repeat. It's a ghost call, I think, because it disappears—then it returns for a time," she said through the com.

"I've picked up the beacon," Bealzabub chimed in. "Cannot triangulate a position in this void. We're screwed, Boss. I think we should try to follow it."

"Real cheerful AI you have, Mr. Brent," said Simon sounding annoyed.

"Let's figure out what it is, shall we?" Helen said, who had quietly entered the bridge. She sat down at the controls and began to work with

Bealzabub. Without a lot of options under the circumstances, Brent went with the only one they had. They tried to follow the sound of the beacon. They were already hopelessly lost. After a time, they gained on the signal, which came and went. Bealzabub caught the signal much better than Helen could.

"I have a reading on the signal, Boss. The SOS is coming from a transport vessel registered as the *Calypso*," the AI said. "I have it on record that this transport met its fate in Jupiter's gravity eighteen months ago—stand by, other details coming online."

"The *Calypso*, I remember hearing about the disaster," Brent said. "The transport got caught somehow and couldn't break free. I don't think anyone survived."

"It's not the *Calypso*, but an escape pod from the *Calypso*," Bealzabub continued. "It seems to be moving at a high velocity on a course toward us. Eighteen minutes."

"Not our business," Simon said. "No one survives out here for eighteen months or even a year. Bloody hell."

"How close will it get to us? Give me the best you can with it; trajectory and velocity," Brent addressed the AI.

"The escape pod is moving at an impressive speed. It approaches 2 percent of the speed of light. It will come within seven kilometres of our vessel."

"Bloody hell—" from Simon again.

"Will you please shut the fuck up, Simon. I'm trying to get us out of this mess," said Brent angrily. "Bub, adjust our heading to intercept the escape pod."

"This isn't a good idea, Brent. the readings are fluctuating wildly. I don't think that the pod is alone out there," Helen said as forcefully as she could.

Brent held his hand up to tell everyone to hold on. He crossed to the console and stooped over it, reading. "What the devil!" he shouted then.

"Turn, turn!" Helen yelled. "WE'RE FLYING INTO A MOUNTAIN!"

"Course correction," Bealzabub said calmly. "Asteroid detected, safety perimeters readjusted. That was a close one, Boss. One of the *Calypso's* escape pods is docked on the asteroid, which, now that the distortion has cleared, is not an asteroid at all but an interstellar class world ship."

The pan system codes read:

Crimson Star 001-0976531

Launch date (Earth Calendar): February 10, 2498 from Neptune Dry Dock

Last transmission received August 11, 2528 – SOS.

2

MAN IN TIME

JOHN PHILIP HENDRICKS, the name he was born with, was only one of the names and titles owned by the man who sat high atop a camel at the head of a procession of nomadic desert warriors. He was the Tyrr, the War Chieftain of the Zingaris, who travelled the lands surrounding the Great Desert, at times even crossing the desert itself. His skin was burnt dark from the extra radiation the sun lines rays were bouncing back up from the sand dunes. He wore the appropriate desert headdress, which was actually more practical than cultural. His eyes were protected by a sun visor, which he had invented himself since taking up life in the desert climate.

Six years ago, when he first came to Terraroma, he hadn't even known that the Zingaris even existed. Now he was their leader. The Zingaris were a nomadic people who had existed in the region that skirted and entered into the Great Desert. They were fierce in battle, and tales spoke of them back in the first revolution when a certain population rose against Magnus Jupiter. They have lived with the desert ever since.

Terraroma was the local name for the world, and this world was the continent-sized circular habitat encased inside an asteroid. Originally called the *Crimson Star*, the McKendree cylinder had been en route to a nearby star system when it became trapped inside a void in timespace. The results had been devastating, and most of the crew was killed outright. The population of the habitat, those who didn't perish in the disaster, had been knocked back to the Stone Age. Time was very different inside of the void; centuries passed and the world continued thanks to the intervention of strange forces. An alien entity, attracted to the ship, merged with the artificial intelligence that was running the habitat. The AI itself had been merged with a desperate commander during the disaster, and the result was a strange triumvirate. The people of the habitat began to climb back up the ladder toward civilization. A society designed after the ancient Roman Republic was created by the AI and later corrupted by the alien. When Hendricks arrived six years earlier, the alien/AI had learned to create humanoid avatars who acted as the leaders, teachers, and finally gods of the people of Terraroma.

"Denzeel," Hendricks said to the man next to him, "call a full stop. This is traditional land. Make for a stopover."

Denzeel, who was dressed much the same, in desert garb, nodded sharply and turned his camel around to face the oncoming procession. He raised his right hand in the universal symbol of stop, and he called out instructions. Strange instruments replied from the distance. The Zingaris would be making camp and laying over for a time. The sun line had moved significantly south. It was early evening, and the light was fading quickly. The area was a traditional camping ground for the Zingaris, and this went back centuries to before the founding of Miceen. They stood on the border of where the grasslands ended and the desert began. They were very close to a spot where, according to legend, the sorceress Olympias had first appeared to travellers. The true history of Terraroma was shrouded in time and legends and mysteries.

Denzeel had grown up believing in all of the legends until one day when strangers arrived in Terraroma. Hendricks and Jones had come to them from somewhere beyond their known world and had changed the whole world in a very short time. Whether those changes were for better or worse was a matter of opinion, which varied depending on who you asked. Revolution was revolution, even in an artificially designed world.

The camp was struck, and Hendricks gave a sigh of relief; everything in this world moved slowly, without the benefit of instant communication satellites or even a telegraph. The stopover was business and as soon as this important meeting was over, the caravan would depart for the Oasis of Tar. There he would see Marianna, daughter of Bester, and the thought of seeing her again was something that made him happier than he had felt in a long time. He made himself comfortable in his own tent and was sending Denzeel away, hoping that his friend would rest some and not worry about him, when he had an afterthought.

"Send old Gais. It's time for another history lesson," Hendricks said, hoping that it sounded like a request and not an order. Denzeel gave a smile and a nod and departed silently. "Old Gais" was an older citizen, late of Miceen who decided to leave the city, as did many, when the reign of the "Good Goddess" rose to replace the reign of Olympias. Gais was what passed for a historian here, and Hendricks was creating a written historical record of Terraroma, something which simply didn't exist before he arrived. Most of the history was passed on verbally, and any written record was always done in the form of commentary.

Tonight he would work with Gais, and they would continue to create a historical timeline for Terraroma, a task Hendricks found oddly satisfying. Tomorrow, perhaps, or at least within the week, he would meet with a delegation from Miceen. They came representing the Good Goddess, who Hendricks knew as Jones, a captain of the peacekeepers who became trapped here with him. Jones and he had tried two find a way back out of this strange world. That was before Captain Jones had sacrificed herself to join with the world-operating AI system as the alien entity was driven out. Had she not done this, the habitat itself might have fallen into disrepair and eventually failed, signalling doomsday for the world of Terraroma.

This was only the third time that Hendricks had communicated with Jones, or the Good Goddess, as the Miceenians referred to her since her transformation. Hendricks had been horrified when he found that his friend had been transformed into this avatar of the hive mind of the Magnus 9 AI system, an ancient commander named Vokova, and the mind and body of Jones herself. In a way, he never reconciled the events of Jones' sacrifice, never forgave her for leaving him here in this mad world. In a way, he thought of Jones as being dead and replaced by a facsimile, but he knew that wasn't exactly true. He had moved on and tried to make a new life here. He'd thought he'd left Jones to her fate, and now she was sending urgent messages. He would listen, but he had no idea what they would have to say to one another.

The Good Goddess rarely left the city limits of Miceen. Hendricks had originally been invited to come to the palace in response to her urgent message, and while the city of Miceen was the hub of civilization in Terraroma, Hendricks wasn't comfortable going there. He had a few crimes to answer for himself lately, and if there was one thing that he had learned in his time in Terraroma, it was simply never to take any unnecessary chances. Shortly after assuming leadership of the Zingaris, he and his band of desert raiders had infringed on territory considered under the protection of the Good Goddess of Miceen. Nothing had come of the incident; Hendricks assumed Jones had let it go because of their history together in Terraroma. His feeling toward his old friend remained complicated.

There was a secondary method for sending messages. The Good Goddess had the ability to speak directly through another person. It was an unnerving experience, and that was likely to be what happened when the Miceenian delegation arrived. Somehow, in some manner that even the AI core didn't understand, the avatar that operated from the matrix— in this case, what remained of Macy Jones—had the ability to project her consciousness into another living person. Hendricks had witnessed this before when the alien entity inhabited the two ruling avatars, but never had he seen it done since Jones sacrificed herself to the matrix. It would be interesting; he had no doubt.

The torches were lit for the evening, and old Gais arrived in short time. Hendricks spent the rest of the evening drinking wine and listening to old legends and tales of the early days of the great civil war in Terraroma. At times, Hendricks was forced to admit to himself that he was happy living here in Terraroma, happy because here he truly felt that he was the master of his own destiny. Free. Freer than he had even felt when he had been travelling around the solar system, chasing after some score or another.

Hendricks sat up straight and smiled at his friend. "I am sorry, old friend, my mind was wandering."

"Again. Your mind was wandering again," Gais said, smiling back at his friend. "I know what you are worried about, Tyrr. You are concerned about the delegation from Miceen that we parlay with soon. This is because of her," he said and stopped talking then, thinking that he had said enough.

They sat silently in Hendricks's tent, which was the largest and most comfortable tent in the camp. Traditionally, other Tyrrs before Hendricks were far more extravagant and loved to display trophies from towns or outposts they had raided. Hendricks lived as the Zingaris lived, by the sword, but he liked to tell himself that he only killed when he had to. He was certainly the most radical leader the Zingaris ever had, but he had won the title fairly in open combat. He had challenged the previous leader because Hendricks was opposed to his unnecessary cruelty in victory. Hendricks had won in single combat and killed the man the old-fashioned way. He had beaten him in a single combat knife fight.

The Zingaris had sworn allegiance to Hendricks as the new Tyrr. They had sworn by the hilt, and in this world, that meant everything.

"Yes, Gais, you are correct. I *am* worried about her, and I'm worried about her connection to the 'spiritual world,' as you would call it. I know her, or maybe I should say that I *knew* her. It was Jones who defeated Olympias, and when she did, there was a void in the system as she pushed the alien entity—Loki, the evil one—out of the collective consciousness of the world." Hendricks paused with a big sigh. He continued. Gais listened politely, nodding now and then, although he was often thrown off by some of the odd comments Hendricks made.

"And Jones understood it, without proper balance of cerebral input in the system, this world would begin to have failures in areas that would be bad for the human population. Jones gave up the life that she once knew to become part of a machine. I know how we debate the word, Gais, but 'machine' is the closest one in both of our vocabularies."

"She is a ghost in a machine, and you said that a machine is an empty thing built by people to serve people. You have said this many times before, Tyrr," Gais said. "But she was your friend, and you fought many battles together; explain to me why you worry."

Hendricks wore a baffled expression. He himself didn't really know why. He tried the best he could to explain his misgivings to the old statesman.

"I suppose that I am concerned that the friend that I knew isn't really there anymore. What she suffered to overcome the alien—uh, the *demon* that had overtaken the system, I can't imagine. I have been there myself, when I fought with Magnus Jupiter, and I discovered that it was the alien, the thing from the void that was controlling events in your world for its own evil reasons. Your history is covered in bloodshed that was perpetuated by that thing. I know you can see this." He paused and looked up at his friend. "I guess I fear that the person I knew won't be there, but a strange imitation of her to speak with me. I find it worrisome that she won't come in person, and I anticipate some magical trick in her place."

"We all have great faith in your leadership, Tyrr. You have changed history in our world in a very short time," Gais said. "They no longer raid the villages or outposts of the Miceenians since so many refugees came to the caravans from Miceen, like myself. People are looking for a new way of life without worshipping these 'rulers.' But, truth be, told they never completely stopped until you became Tyrr. Many ask, where will we ride if peace reigns over the south?"

"It's a big world, Gais," Hendricks said with a smile. He laughed to himself at how astonishingly huge this McKendree cylinder actually was, a stunning fact that he didn't think he'd ever stop being awed by. "We could go north, then. Why not? I've heard some pretty stupid stories floating around. Ghost warriors hiding in the wastes?" Hendricks said with a smirk.

"Well, when you get to my age, you start taking those ghost stories more seriously," Gais said with a laugh.

Hendricks laughed too and reached for more wine.

3

REUNION

THE TIME CAME at last to meet the Miceenian delegation, and Hendricks could see them approach from the southeast. The idea was for the group to arrive before the hottest point in the day; it was quite comfortable in the oasis in which they were camped, but they were still close to the Great Desert, an uninhabitable desert wasteland that had been formed when disaster struck the world ship. That had been ages ago, of course, and Hendricks was stating a theory based on information from the AI mind that ran the environments of Terraroma. During his fateful battle with Magnus Jupiter those many years ago, he had a brief interaction with the strange matrix that ran the world ship. He had encountered the surviving spirit of the *Crimson Star*'s original commander, a man named Vokova, and he had learned many things about how the interior lands were formed during the great disaster.

Off in the distance, he saw the Miceenians approached in their Roman-style military march. This was a cohort out of the ninth legion; the most revered in the Miceenian army; these were handpicked soldiers who often served the personal guard for the Good Goddess. Hendricks had once marched in their ranks, as had Denzeel, who was now riding out to meet them. He would deliver a scroll with a formal invitation to meet at a designated spot and join him later in his tent for dinner. He doubted that anyone was in a hurry to sit down in his tent with him for dinner; the Miceenians were pretty xenophobic, and they had all kinds of misconceptions about desert people.

Hendricks made his way through the Zingaris' camp toward his tent, where Denzeel would meet him with the reply. From there, they would go to the parlay itself. Denzeel was Hendricks's most trusted adviser and, as such, Denzeel always accompanied Hendricks if there was a parlay to attend. In the time since he had become Tyrr, the nomadic tribe had increased its numbers significantly and had made allies and established trade in a way that was new to the tribe. It was simple. Hendricks merely negotiated with those that they encountered and often avoided violence. Most of the time, things worked out, but there were always those exceptions. Death, it seemed, was part of life here in Terraroma.

"Looks like you were right about them not wanting to stay for dinner, Tyrr," Denzeel said as soon as he entered the tent. Denzeel had a slightly lopsided smile which he displayed having said that; he grew up in Miceenian culture and wasn't offended by the refused courtesy as some of the desert tribe would be.

"Just as well," Hendricks said. "I really don't feel like sitting around and posturing when I know that whatever Jones has to say at the beginning will be all that is important." *And it won't even be Jones who actually talks, but some priestess channelling her voice,* he thought, glumly. Another little trick that the Good Goddess has picked up was the ability to project herself through another person; he had no idea how that worked but it was a very useful tool politically.

Hendricks and Denzeel proceeded to the designated spot for the parlay, a small group of warriors trailed behind them. The fighters would hang back at a respectable distance from the meeting, as would the priestess' bodyguards. Both escorts stood at attention, although the Zingaris seemed much more comfortable in their desert dress than the Miceenians in their heavy battle helmets and thick leather breastplates. Hendricks had to hide a smile as he passed a sweating centurion. An open tent with comfortable chairs and a small table was set up for the two parties to sit and discuss whatever the issue was. The parlay had been called by the Good Goddess and the Council of Miceen. This was a rare occasion, indeed, and while the Zingaris and the Miceenians were not enemies, they were not allies, either.

Hendricks stood behind his chair, Denzeel to his right, and they greeted Priestess Helena and her companion. The other woman was not a priestess; she was a soldier and obviously the bodyguard for Helena. After the formalities were dispensed with, they all sat.

Priestess Helena spoke. "Please allow me a moment to prepare; you understand that the Good Goddess will speak to you through me, and I need a moment to let her spirit enter me. She is close to me. I can feel her near. it will be soon." Helena was a dark-haired woman with classical Asian features; she was perhaps in her late fifties, although it was hard to guess a person's age in Terraroma. Lifespan tended to vary between the '80s to the early 120s, which in fact wasn't that different from the lifespan of the average citizen in the Sol System at the time of the *Crimson Star*'s departure. The people living within Terraroma did not have the medical advances that modern system citizens enjoyed. Back in the modern society Hendricks had been born into, a person could expect to live to 150 years.

Helena sat quietly for a few moments and forced her breathing to slow. Her complexion began to change, and it suddenly appeared as if her face were lit with green light. She sat still and rigid for a moment longer with her eyes closed. Finally, her body relaxed in the chair and her eyes opened.

"Hello again, Mr. Hendricks," Helena's mouth spoke, but the voice was that of a different woman; it was the voice of Macy Jones with some odd synthetic inflections. "Hello, John, and hello, Denzeel, it is good to see you again." This time the voice completely resembled the voice of Macy Jones, the woman Hendricks had come to Terraroma with many years earlier. To himself, Hendricks thought of her as the multiple personality goddess. She was, after all, part of a kind of hive mind, a collective of an ancient commander, the ship's AI system, and Jones's mind.

As the person of Priestess Helena spoke, the voice and personality changed, sometimes quickly, sometimes one voice taking over for a time.

"We have asked for this parlay because there is trouble coming to Terraroma." The voice was male, Russian. This was the voice of Commander Vokova, the first human to successfully join with the AI system that ran the *Crimson Star*; Hendricks had met Vokova's consciousness years earlier, while Hendricks was trapped in an eerie stasis. Vokova had helped Hendricks to break free and return to the ordinary world. "We, together, represent the majority of free people and have an obligation to act in light of recent events."

Hendricks bent forward slightly before he spoke. He generally hated politics but in this upside-down world, politics were often plain madness. "You already know that I have a pax with Marcellus, and I know that Miceen and Augustine have had a very strained peace since the Fall of the Giants. What now has changed that the Zingaris should act?"

"Something has changed. Marcellus has been declared to be a god." The voice was Jones this time. "And it's worse than that. I've suspected for some time that Loki is still alive. Now we are seeing events for the first time that give me pause." Here, the voice of Jones paused, and then the voice of Vokova took over.

"Loki lives. He has seduced General Marcellus by playing on the man's big, fat ego. I have never seen a human relish in ambition the way that man does. Yes, Mr. Hendricks, we can observe events at times, and we have seen him change in most unnatural ways. I saw his lust for power grow as he marched on Augustine all those years ago."

"I told you then that I could not destroy the alien we call Loki, but that he was driven out—out of the system." This was Jones's voice now. "What happened to the thing then? Did it go out into space, into the void that it came from?" Hendricks almost imagined Jones shuddering as she said this, but that was a silly notion. The real Jones, or whatever was left of her, had been synthesized and absorbed into the great AI that ran this world. She existed within an avatar copy of Jones's physical self. This woman before him was a vessel, and the voices were the psychic echoes of people who were not really human anymore. He didn't want to think of Jones that way, but it was hard not to after she'd sacrificed herself in that final battle with the alien within the Olympias avatar.

"So," said Hendricks, "you believe that the vile thing is still here in Terraroma, wandering around like an evil spirit and somehow manipulating Marcellus, possessing him, even, to do Loki's bidding?" Hendricks was well aware that Marcellus had reacted aggressively when he'd learned of the new Good Goddess taking control in Miceen after the fall of Olympias. To Hendricks, it was just more of the same—some magical god-figure telling everyone what to do. A strange peace had hung over Terraroma since Hendricks had taken leadership of the Zingaris, a direct result of the new balance of power. Were the Zingaris to back either city in a new war, the balance of power would be shifted.

"You do not understand. We have come to warn you of Marcellus." The Russian accent this time. "Loki has merged with Marcellus, body and soul. Loki is like a worm, and his invasion of Marcellus was cunning and slow as the thing worked its way into his mind. Marcellus would not know where his thoughts started and the alien thing's ended. He has reopened the sports of war; gladiators die in the arena every week in New Augustine. You see how it lusts for pain and suffering and blood?"

The woman, Helena, who was physically doing the talking, was beginning to show signs of stress and a short recess was called. Denzeel pulled Hendricks to the side and asked him if he had any idea where this was going. What did the Miceenians want? Was war between the two cities once again inevitable? Could the Zingaris tip the balance of power? Hendricks listened to his friend and adviser, but said nothing.

As they resumed, Hendricks said, "How can the Zingaris be of assistance? Jones, if you really are still in there, then you can't want war. You know what that means and who would want to go that way if there was another choice?"

"This is not about what anyone wants, Mr. Hendricks. How long do you think it will be before Marcellus wants to march south again? He is crucifying anyone who disagrees with him in Augustine. There is no doubt left that it is Loki who is really in control and, Hendricks, there is something else."

There was a worrisome urgency in the words. Hendricks realized that this parlay was anything but straightforward. "Don't keep me in suspense," he said bitterly.

The intonations were mainly Vokova now when the priestess spoke again. "A ship has docked on the west side of the *Crimson Star*. Yes, another ship has become lost in this void in space and has come here. It is a small trader-class ship with three people aboard. Loki is well aware of the fact, so Marcellus has dispatched soldiers to go and get the crew."

Hendricks was truly shocked. This was probably the only news that he hadn't been prepared to hear. He could have predicted almost anything in this strange world, but he hadn't expected anyone else to wander into this trap. "Well, we'd better get after them before it's too late!" he exclaimed.

"It is already too late. Somehow Loki had a jump on us. Marcellus's soldiers will reach them soon, well before we could get there. We need another plan."

"What?" Hendricks exclaimed. "The damn thing was purged from the system, you said. How could it know another ship's docked? How can it see?"

"I don't know." Low intonations of Jones's voice. "But this has me worried very much."

The meeting carried on for some time after that, and frequent breaks were needed to help the priestess cope with the extended interface of mind and body. Finally, after much unexpected conversation, a plan of action was agreed upon. Denzeel and the soldier who had accompanied the priestess joined in the planning and eventually, after the talk ended, both parties left quickly to make preparations for the upcoming action. Hendricks had agreed to form a recon party to find the people from the trader. It went without saying that he would never trust anyone else to deal with this situation. He and Denzeel would be riding out to adventure once again.

4

BLINDSIDED

WHEN THEY STEPPED out of the *Maryjane,* they were all well armed; Helen had a disrupter and a taser whip, Simon had a laser pistol and a palm knife, but Brent was truly armed to the teeth. He had a military-grade laser rifle with three firing options, a laser pistol on one hip, a handy automatic handgun on the other, and, finally, a modern replica of an ancient bayonet strapped to his boot. When the small trader was brought in to the dock by automatic docking sensors, Helen tried to get readings on what was waiting for them when the doors opened, but something had infiltrated their AI as soon as they were locked in. Bealzabub was not heard from again.

Nothing was there when the doors opened. A shuttle pod, not unlike an elevator, stood open and waiting for the new arrivals. They rode it to their next destination, again prepared to fight if necessary when the pod stopped wherever it was taking them. Simon grumbled about being in such close quarters, a clear tactical disadvantage.

Again, nothing and no one there when the doors opened. They walked down an empty corridor. The overhead track lights followed them as they moved ever toward an unknown destination that lay somewhere farther down the darkened passage.

"Everything is on automatic," said Simon. "Where is the crew of this vessel? Is everyone inside of the habitat, maybe the AI hasn't told anyone that it brought us in."

"Don't forget how impossibly huge this place is. The world ships took decades to build. The design and execution of the original plans has been compared to the building of the great cathedrals in Europe on Earth in the Middle Ages. It was a whole new generation that finally launched the interstellar class ships out into the void between the solar systems. This one, the *Crimson Star,* was the first to be commissioned and the last to be finished. Oh, and it was the biggest of them all," Brent said as they continued on their way, chasing the darkness.

"Didn't know that you were such a historian, Mr. Brent." said Helen. She wore a worried expression on her attractive face; it had disturbed her deeply when the trader's AI went down. She had been interfaced with Bealzabub when the attack came. That was the only way to describe it, an attack. The *Crimson Star*'s AI seemed to scan the trader and then extend a friendly status.

As the two AI systems met, she felt something strange happen; nothing like this had ever happened to her before. The world ship's AI was in a different class altogether than Bealzabub. Suddenly, Helen had felt cold, like someone was pouring ice water into her head.

The trader started to power down and its systems were rapidly turned off one by one. There was little time to spare, and Brent was out of his mind, worried that this was going to end badly for all of them. She wanted to tell them that she felt like the trader ship was at least partly purged. She didn't know if Bealzabub was purged, but it was certainly harshly disconnected from her wetware.

Finally, they found a passage that led deeper into the ship and discovered a habitat access port. The room was almost empty, and lights and a ventilation system started up when they entered. Stale air blew in their faces for a few minutes, bringing curses from Simon until it finally ran clear.

In a short time, Helen was able to override the lock system and they gained access to the contamination hub. Moments later, the far port—a large circular door—hissed and popped open. They stepped through and air, the freshest air any of them had smelled in a long time, filled their lungs. They were in a shallow cave, which was illuminated by something like diffused sunlight.

As they stood at the lip of the cave, they looked out onto a new world unlike any of them had ever seen before. A steep incline of heavily wooded land stretched out before them, and in the great distance beyond, through mist and cloud and glare, the far end of the horizon bent upward until it disappeared beyond the limit of human sight. The world curved over on itself as the slow spin created gravity upon the lands inside. In the other direction, it was a stunning sight to behold, and all three of them stood still, gazing out for a time. Far into the hazy distance, a massive body of water could be seen; the iron-grey waters of some inland sea hung at some impossible angle.

Finally, Brent broke the spell. "All right, let's go and find someone," he said, looking a bit more assured than he had in a while. They began their way down the hills, making their way around the more heavily wooded parts of the slope until they finally came to more level terrain. As they were moving downhill, they were also moving toward the horizon, which stretched up into the place where the sky should be. The effect was overwhelming for the newcomers; Simon couldn't help but try to see what was "ahead" by looking up at a certain angle. It was a futile effort when one realized that one was looking at the signs of a landscape that was many, many kilometres away. The "sky" was a mass of diffused, milky yellow light and cloud. No one could actually see the far side of the cylinder, but people couldn't help but try when they first entered the habitat.

"Helen, can you detect any kind of signals in here? People must be using some type of communications. This place is like a small continent," Brent said. He shielded his eyes from the glare and pivoted, trying to get a fix on their surroundings.

"No, Brent, nothing. Either something is shielding everything from me, or no one in here is using any tech at all. There is a weird background signal that is too strong for my software, but otherwise, I don't think that anyone in here is using any tech," Helen said, almost sounding embarrassed. "When we first came in, I had all the channels in my head open, and it was all empty except for some kind of electronic backdrop that I've never heard before."

"That's crazy," Brent replied.

"If you think that's crazy, Mr. Brent, you'd best take a look at what's coming. Check your six," said Simon. Even as he spoke, the others noticed the sound of soldiers marching. The heat from the sun line was burning off the mist, and they could see who was marching toward them.

Brent shook his head and looked again; approaching from about 50 yards were ancient Roman soldiers. There was an entire group of them in block formation, marching seven across and maybe five deep. The man in charge, presumably, was the guy with the coloured plume across the top of his helm. The soldiers were outfitted pretty much the way they looked back in Brent's history classes. They wore chest plates of light bronze or hardened leather. One man carried a long pole with an eagle standard shining proudly at the top. They carried short swords and shields, and looked a great deal meaner than the holograms he'd seen in school. Their leader barked out some unintelligible orders, and they broke rank quickly, taking up new positions surrounding Brent and his companions.

"Surrender yourselves in the name of Marcellus Saturanius Rex, who is called Great Saturn now," said the commander of the group. "Throw down your weapons and try no magic upon us. We know of you."

"We are looking for someone who is in charge of this world ship," Brent said forcefully, showing no fear when he was certainly feeling it.

Simon had his weapons drawn while Helen was still staring with her mouth hanging open. At first, she was concerned that she was the only woman in this scene and then noticed that some of the soldiers that surrounded them were in fact women. That wasn't like any Romans she ever read about. Was this some kind of historical festival or re-enactment or something?

"Great Saturn has warned me that you might try to bewitch us with strange words. Surrender your arms to us now and we will take you before his divinity," the commander said firmly. His soldiers took a step closer.

Helen activated her taser whip. She let it roll out from her hand like a long electric blue chord. Sparks snapped from its end, causing some of the closest soldiers alarm. *They're acting like they never saw a taser whip before,* Helen thought, then realized, *no, they're acting like they've never seen electricity before.*

"Great Saturn bade me to approach you peacefully; you must accompany us to the great city of Necropolis, which was once called Augustine. If you refuse, I am to take you anyway," The commander said firmly and placed his hand on the hilt of his sword.

"Look, we don't understand what's going on here and we're sure not going to surrender to anyone," Brent said again, and as if on cue, the soldiers came at them.

A tall female soldier walked right up to Helen and tried to grab the wrist the taser whip was in. Helen resisted, and the soldier smashed into her with shield, easily knocking her to the ground. Then all hell broke loose.

Brent yelled out to leave her alone at the same time as Simon drew his laser pistol and shot the soldier who had pushed Helen down. The laser shot was a clean, hot hit in the shoulder; it burnt through the armour easily enough and went straight through her shoulder. The soldier screamed in pain and fell to the ground. Simon was re-aiming his pistol at the commander of the group now, and as fast as he did, another soldier quickly stepped up with his short heavy sword drawn and hacked Simon's right hand clear off. He howled in pain.

Brent couldn't believe what was happening to them. It was insane. It was impossible, but it was happening. He had the laser rifle level, and he fired off a special taser blast; everyone in front of him for about 20 degrees was shocked significantly and thrown backwards. This bought him a few moments to try to help Simon.

"I'm done for. I'm bleeding—help me!" Simon cried out as he tried to stop the blood gushing out of his arm. Brent unlocked his own laser pistol and, quickly as he could, he used the heat setting to cauterize the end of Simon's arm. It worked; the bleeding stopped and Simon's stump smoked for a few moments before he passed out from shock and pain.

As this was going on, other soldiers were trying to arrest Helen as she was getting back to her feet. She used the taser whip, the end wrapping around an approaching soldier's leg and the electrical shock making his nervous system go haywire for time. He went down, and another kicked Helen from behind, knocking her off balance. A third soldier came in with his sword drawn and would have killed Helen if Brent hadn't stopped it all.

"Enough!" he cried. "We surrender!" Then he threw down his laser rifle. It wasn't the worst tactic. All modern weapons—electronic ones, at least—were personalized to the owner, and no one but the owner could activate the weapon. These people couldn't use the weapons against them. However, now they were surrounded by swords and spears.

"Where is the commander of the *Crimson Star*?" Brent tried again to get answers in this madness. The commanding soldier walked up to Brent and stared straight at him. There was a blankness in the commander's eyes that frightened Brent.

"None of that, I said!" the commander yelled and cracked Brent in the head with the hilt of his sword.

Brent fell unconscious.

They had arrived in Terraroma.

5

SATURN RISING

WHEN BRENT CAME to that first night, he was lying on his face in the back of a horse-drawn wagon. A caged wagon. He rolled over onto his back, and the first thing he thought was, *I can see stars. How can that be? We're inside the galaxy's largest tin can.*

Later on, he would reason out that he had seen a very clever holographic star show of the stars as seen from Earth. Brent had been an avid stargazer from a very young age; he knew how to navigate his hover scooter around any of the Great Lakes on Earth by the time he was seventeen, entirely by the stars. The Great Lakes were a bit different in Brent's time, as old mother Earth had to deal with centuries of the human race destroying everything it came into contact with. The great environmental crash of the early twenty-second century had made some alterations to most of the globe by 2140. While these thoughts were all just ancient history, the fact remained that Brent knew his stars, and knew the sky he was looking at must be a clever simulation.

His head hurt like hell. Inside the wagon with him were Simon and Helen, but both appeared asleep at the moment. The wagon bumped and lurched through the night. What the hell had they gotten themselves into here? This was madness; they have been assaulted and taken prisoner by a bunch of insane men, or barbarians, or both!

What was this strange world and what had happened to the crew? If he had been alone, Brent might have thought he'd gone mad—space happy, if those stories were true. But he wasn't alone; Helen and Simon had experienced the same thing. Simon had even lost his goddamned hand!

The next three days were about as miserable as they could be as they travelled to their destination. The commander made sure they were fed and given water and whatever reasonable things that a prisoner could hope for. A doctor came to see Simon about his severed hand, which surprised Brent and Helen. A bent old man in a dirty toga examined Simon's wrist and was shocked at how well the wound was healing. The clean, quick cauterization that Brent had done had closed the main artery and fried the ends of the nerves off. Simon, himself, had been uncharacteristically quiet for him as they rode to meet their abductor. Helen and Brent did their best to discuss the predicament that they were in.

"It's a goddamn nightmare is what this is," Brent said in a low voice.

Simon, who had his back to them as he constantly peered out of the wagon at the passing landscape, twisted his head around and laughed. "You've driven yer little ship straight into hell. And that's where we're going, people. We are hell-bound."

"Keep your voice down." Helen hissed at Simon. She turned to Brent. "Something has gone wrong on this world ship. Maybe it happened a long time ago. I heard that they lost touch with the *Crimson Star* after it had been out in the void between the star systems for decades. Some kind of mass psychosis, maybe? I heard about a colony where they all went mad and when the authorities found the place, 60 percent of the population had been eaten by the survivors."

"That doesn't fit, Helen. Look at these people. They're not running around foaming at the mouth. They are well-ordered in their action, but they seem to think we're on the Italian peninsula, 2,000 years ago. Or some goddamned thing. It's insane." Brent's head felt better, but he was still weak.

They continued to speak, Brent and Helen mostly. Brent was worried about Simon; he wasn't handling the situation well, if there was a right way to handle losing a hand. Brent and Helen decided that it was better to use this time to rest and gather strength for whatever was next, rather than attempt an escape. Simon ignored them and kept to himself.

The odds were against them right now. Maybe they could reason with whatever passed for authority there.

Little else changed for the duration of the journey to the city they were headed toward. The wagon they were imprisoned in was covered on top but had hard wooden rungs, which were thatched across the sides.

They could see out and were utterly stunned when they saw the city of Necropolis. The size and apparent population were immense. The architecture was classic Greco-Roman style with the odd modern trick thrown in. They saw an overarching passageway that could never have held up if it was constructed from classical, natural sources. Modern microfibres were being used here somehow.

What really disturbed Brent were the people. He liked to think that he was a pretty good judge of character and could evaluate the mood of a group or a crowd, but the folks they passed in the streets were odd. Usually, the average citizen is a pretty peace-loving person and the cops or soldiers could be any degree of killer, but in here, it looked like anyone was capable of murder. Even the young and old had a vicious look and carried knives and other weapons. Cruel eyes watched from shadowy corners; distant laughter sounded mean. This was not a healthy population, like Berlin under the Nazis in the twentieth century or the USA under Cleever about a hundred years later. History had enough examples of how low human behaviour could go under the wrong circumstances, and Brent was pretty sure that was what he was seeing here—the results of iron-fisted oppression.

Eventually, it appeared that they had reached their destination. The horse and wagon stopped in front of a palace with many sentries standing at their posts. The structure looked as though it had been constructed to accommodate larger-than-human proportions, and it also appeared that the place had suffered significant damage sometime in the past. War? That would seem to be the obvious answer, considering what they'd seen so far.

"Let me do the talking, okay?" Brent said to the others, but he was mainly concerned with Simon, who had a most unreadable expression on his face. Brent's personal experience with the man was limited to the job they had been on together. Simon's reputation in the business of moving contraband was solid; however, the circumstances that they found themselves in were far from ordinary, even in the sketchy business that they were used to. How was one expected to react to having a hand chopped off and then being taken prisoner by a group of people acting like ancient Romans? The only thing Brent knew for certain was the look on Simon's face told him the man wasn't handling things well.

Crowds of citizens stood far back behind security parameters as the three prisoners were led up long steps and through tall, wooden double doors. With centurions on either side of them, they strode down a long hallway of marble. They had to step around chunks of marble and plaster. Busts of previous celebrated citizenry once adorned this hallway. Now they were all smashed to pieces. *That sent a message to the people, no doubt*, Brent thought bitterly as they were ushered farther into the palace. They came to two large brass doors, with a man on each side to open them. As they did so, a cool but unpleasant-smelling draft escaped from the doors. A place that was closed up too long, too often.

One of the guards pushed Simon through the doors and the other guards caught on. Brent and Helen were all pushed and shoved until the three of them had gone deep into the shadowy hall. The chamber was badly lit by low, burning lamps hanging on large marble pillars. Shadows and flicking firelight played cat and mouse around the walls.

In a regal-looking chair with a high back and extensive armrests atop a slightly raised dais, a largely built man sat in shadow. He looked up as the strangers were led into the chamber. When they were at a respectable distance, the man rose from his seat and the guards stopped. They all went down on one knee, while saluting with the right arm.

"Hail Great Saturn!" they shouted in unison.

Brent and his crew neither bowed nor saluted upon seeing the man, obviously the authority here. They stood and looked at him. He was exceptionally tall compared to most of the others they had encountered. The man was a warrior, himself; tall and powerfully built with a few telltale battle scars. The strangest aspect of the man was that his face appeared to be older than the rest of him. He had deep-set, bloodshot eyes that seemed cruel as they stared out and scanned the newcomers. The skin of his face was slightly darker and weathered-looking.

"It is customary to kneel in the presence of a god," said the man called Saturn.

Simon went down, stumbling slightly, on one knee. Helen and Brent looked at each other for a moment, and then Brent spoke. "It is our custom to make new friends by meeting as equals. We seek the highest authority on this sh— ... uh, in your society," he said as reasonably as he could.

Saturn laughed aloud at this. "You are from the outside and will have to learn our ways. Welcome to Terraroma, Mr. Brent. I am afraid I know only your name." He came closer and they saw that he was dressed much the same as a soldier, only his uniform was made from silk and gold and finer leather than they had seen on the common soldiers. He approached Simon, who was still kneeling, saying, "This man has a much more respectful attitude. He will do well here with us, I think."

Brent watched the man called Saturn for long moments and knew somehow, perhaps by instinct, that there was something unnatural about this person. He could not exactly see what it was, but whatever it was, it made him nervous and fearful in a primal way. *Is this evil?* Brent was a twenty-sixth-century man and didn't think in those terms as a rule, but the feeling was there. There was a friendly, even compelling sensation, but deeper beneath was a sensation of fear and panic.

"I am the highest authority that you are ever going to meet because it is my destiny to rule all of Terraroma. You have come from the outside and you bring with you knowledge—that is part of my fate—you may achieve glory with me by assisting me to rebuild the lost arts I once wielded as Magnus Jupiter. That was long ago," Saturn said, trailing off and sounding unsure for a moment.

"You want us to help you!" Helen burst in. "First, we're docked against our will, then assaulted and kidnapped and now you think we should be happy to help you play Caesar or whatever you're doing in here. The fuck with that."

Helen's sudden aggressive tone caught Brent off guard, and he attempted to compensate with what he thought was a more reasonable approach. "This is a world ship called the *Crimson Star*. It was launched from Neptune dry dock and became lost..."

"Shut up!" Saturn bellowed in a voice loud enough to echo off the walls. Brent and Helen flinched while Simon and the guards cringed. "I heard enough of that when I had to listen to Vokova. I will destroy Vokova one day, and you will help me. But first, it seems you need to learn the discipline of the temple!"

Saturn clapped his hands after the last command, and Brent and his crew were dragged away again. This time, they were separated, taken beneath the palace, and led into a dungeon that had many ugly rooms and solitary cells. Brent heard anguished moans and sometimes outright screams issue from dark and unseen corners. A cold, dark, and dimly lit solitary cell was where he ended up. He was certain that none of the cries he heard came from either of his companions. Eventually, a guard brought water and bread. Finally, there was nothing to do but rest.

At least a day passed, but then, again, time always passed strangely in a dungeon. Brent slept when he could but was often lost in a half-dream state that was different and yet the same as reality. Sleep was fitful and unpleasant, so he forced himself into consciousness and waited for whatever was next to come along. It seemed like a long wait, but at last a guard came and collected him. He was taken back to what he thought of as the throne room.

The guards unchained him and left him there alone. He was wondering about Helen and Simon when Saturn made his entrance from a shadowy corner of the large room. Saturn lit a lantern, and Brent saw what looked like the ruins of some technical equipment. What looked like a modified biobed was there; medical application that seemed to have been modified but also damaged. Burnt tubes and scars from some great source of heat. Brent was becoming accustomed to more shocking information all the time now, but this was getting really strange. A modified medical biobed in a Roman throne room?

"When I say that you come from outside, Mr. Brent, I mean that you are visiting in my realm of space. I was afloat in the universe like a boat on a stormy sea but without the senses that we enjoy in this world. No light, no dark, no time! Suddenly something split then from now and this world—what you called *Crimson Star* and we call Terraroma—was before me. Somehow, I *felt* it's distress and I *heard* its gods calling out for help. I entered this world then and I met the gods of this world, Magnus 9 and Vokova." As he spoke, Saturn strode about the room; his movements seemed uncertain, as if he were rehearsing a part in a play.

"I did not understand how you communicated with each other, but I felt the waves of emotion, and they intoxicated me." He gave a sudden overly dramatic gesture with his arms and continued. "I was more than happy to help and together, we saved this place and *order* was returned. I learned from the two gods here, and we became three. I revelled in the emotions of the people in this world—fear and pain, horror and hate, so delicious! Time is different here, I understand, and I wanted to learn more about the big buzzing rock in space. The place where you all came from. The place called Earth."

"You're an alien!" Brent said as if it was the first thing to make sense in a long time.

Saturn tilted his head to the side as if considering this. "Well, yes, I suppose I am. But this is a human body that I'm living in; I have learned so much from taking this body. This was General Marcellus once, just as I was Loki once. Now I am Saturn. Change is part of life for my species, and we are few."

Brent stared closely at the man. He remembered a fantasy show as a child with the character Hercules, and this person looked like the character. Built like a tank with a magnanimous smile and short fuse, Brent was willing to bet. The man was tall, with salt and pepper grey hair. His face was weathered and partly covered with a small brown beard. Only the eyes didn't fit the legend; they were sunken and bleary, at best. Dead and vacant. Haunted.

It was time to get to the point.

"Where are my crew, and what do you want with us?" Brent said. If he could talk his way out of this mess, it would be a miracle. From committing high crimes against the system to landing in freak land, it was turning out to be a bad week.

"Good," said Saturn. "That's the way to do it. Straight to the point. I was once part of the intelligence that runs this world. I was helping the population climb up out of barbarism so that they might worship me without fear or hesitation. This is my right, to be nourished by the delicacies of emotion that the people emanate." Saturn gestured to the medical biobed and other equipment in the corner of the throne room.

"If you can assist me in repairing the portal equipment which give me direct access to the main system, I promise you a life of pleasure and easy living. And you could sit in my council of advisers, if you have the ambition for that. Consider this carefully."

"Maybe I just want to go back to my ship?"

"It is my ship now," Saturn said and took two swift steps closer to Brent. He was at least three inches taller than Brent and a great deal wider. Brent knew how to keep cool under pressure, and while this situation was stranger than most, the principle was the same; never let them see you sweat.

"Yeah? Buddy, if you don't know any better, that ship isn't going anywhere for anyone but me. Just go ahead and try to take her for a spin, see what good it does you." Brent said defiantly.

Saturn knew how to play poker, too; he just walked around a bit, smiling at his captive out of the corner of his eye like a cat deciding when to take a bird. "I have no need to take your ship anywhere, Mr. Brent. It is sufficient that I deprive you of access to it."

"You drive a shitty deal, man. You will get no help from me," Brent said flatly.

Saturn scowled at him and abruptly turned his back to him. "Guards," he called out, "take this fool down to the coliseum and give him to Gerard. See if the master of the games can do something with him down there."

The guards were on him fast enough, and Brent was dragged away from the palace then. Brent knew enough about ancient Roman culture to have a pretty good idea of what kind of fate awaited him at the coliseum. Death in combat in front of a cheering crowd of sick fucks. Or maybe they would make him fight some animal, like a lion or something. Either way, that didn't seem like it would work out very well. He had no idea about his crew. They were all stuck here in this mad world that made no sense. *How could this be the same world ship that we knew about? What the hell happened here?*

When they arrived, he was taken to a cell with a small, barred window that looked out onto the main field of the coliseum; he was going to get to watch it happen to others before he went out there himself. He wondered about Simon and Helen. *Where did they get taken to? Would Saturn do the same with them? Try and bargain for some kind of technical help that I don't understand the purpose of.*

Finally, he lay down to rest and prepare himself for whatever was ahead for him. Tomorrow was coming fast enough.

6

LET THE GAMES BEGIN

WHEN BRENT AWOKE, he took a better look at the cell he was in. A small hole had been knocked into one wall, maybe intentionally, from the dimensions of it. Not enough room to escape from, but it supplied a view of the arena; a large circular dirt floor, stands that could hold a sizable crowd, and large iron gates on the far side. This was just the kind of psychological torture that he would have expected from the man he'd met last night. And it was working very well, thank you very much. Time crawled that day in the cell, and ugly anticipation when night fell—he was guessing at time—and he saw men setting up the arena for coming entertainment.

He sat in the cell and tried to calm himself; fear was the biggest enemy to defeat. Many things that would seem unlikely or surprising arise when someone beats fear. They defy the odds, and that's what he intended to do. Brent was a determined and sometimes stubborn person, and he wasn't going to die in there.

He rose from his relaxed position when he heard the sound of people coming into the coliseum. He watched as the stands filled up; music floated in the air, vendors hocked their wares, and the people chatted quietly while they waited for the event to begin. The people all looked very Roman in their dress and manner. They were, however, made up of all the races of the human species. A special covered box seat was set high up so Saturn could address the crowd if he wished. The special seating was large enough to accommodate a few VIPs and assorted lackeys. Saturn arrived in good fashion and declared the event open.

Two contests passed and Brent began to relax, thinking perhaps he would not be thrust out there tonight. The first match was badly paired, and the stronger man displayed great cruelty as he dragged out the fight for the crowd. The second was better, but it was more awkward looking than he imagined; Brent had never seen anyone killed with a sword before. This was an education in insanity.

"We have something special tonight!" Saturn bellowed from his seat. He was standing, and Brent could see him gesturing toward the iron gates below and to his right. "We have something out of this world; a would-be invader from lands beyond the Great Mountains! A true villain with tricks aplenty." Saturn laughed at his little joke and the hoards of sycophants all laughed too, just a bit off cue.

Brent's head started to spin before he actually understood what was happening.

The iron gates at the far end of the arena opened and a familiar figure was thrust out into the field. Helen!

Brent watched in vain as the crowd began to cheer at what he did not know. Still hit with the shock of seeing Helen there, he slowly realized that Helen's opponent had entered the arena from his end of the field. Finally, he came into view, a big barrel of a man who had 150 pounds on Helen, strutting around and mugging for the crowd. As the cheers died down, the two combatants faced each other. The big man, whose name the crowd yelled, "Gore"—had for himself a small shield and a heavy-looking double-bladed axe. Helen had a decent-sized shield and a long sword suited to her size. Saturn gave a signal, and some kind of brass instruments blasted to call the start of the fight.

The second the start was called, Helen began to run straight at Gore, who was still a good distance away. Gore caught on and began to lumber toward Helen at the best speed he could muster. As the two grew closer, Helen threw her shield aside and pulled her sword in tight. Closer and closer they came, with neither stopping to adopt a defensive stance. Gore's axe was held high in anticipation. At the optimum moment with perfect timing, Helen dropped down low and slid between Gore's legs.

She delivered a hammer punch to his testicles. Gore howled in pain and anger as Helen slid past to safety; she rolled once and came up with her sword drawn.

Brent watched his shipmate display fighting skills he hadn't known she had. He was pleasantly surprised and suddenly hopeful that they might survive and escape this place.

Gore was quick to recover and was on the attack now; in an amazing display of strength, he spun his axe in a blinding loop as he pressed toward Helen. She stood her ground and parried like a fencer, jabbing forward. After a few moments of this, Helen beat his guard. Gore howled a curse as her jab cut his forearm and his axe flew from his grasp.

The crowd let out a gasp of surprise. Gore stumbled about, swinging his shield as if it were a weapon and by doing so, let down his guard. Helen moved fast to exploit the opening. With a quick step, she sliced the back of Gore's knee and he fell to the ground. And with that, Helen had the tip of her sword at Gore's eye. She had him.

The crowd roared, some booing, some cheering. Brent tried to call out to Helen, but she couldn't hear him. Saturn was standing in his balcony now, and the crowd—who had been calling out their own verdict on Gore—fell silent to see what the lord and master thought. Saturn grinned savagely as he displayed a clear thumbs-down sign. Brent could not have imagined him giving any other decision.

Helen looked up at Saturn for a moment, then dropped the sword and walked away toward the gate through which she had entered. The crowd booed, Gore hurled insults, and Brent wondered what Saturn would do, if he would punish her somehow. Saturn shrugged but wore a disapproving expression. It was clear to everyone that Helen simply refused to execute the man. Ultimately, Saturn did nothing, and the rest of the event seemed like a haze to Brent. He kept wondering if he'd see Simon next. *Would Saturn put a man with one hand in the arena?* he wondered. Well, probably, but Simon did not appear.

Another day passed with little event. There were many others being held here; some came in for the games, and some were there merely to be executed. Brent was made to spar with other fighters, but not with those who were deemed to be gladiators. This title only belonged to a few elite fighters who had survived many seasons of competition. As far as he could learn, there were four major gladiatorial houses in the city of Augustine. These were large estates where people, slaves, were trained to fight as gladiators in the arena. There were other cities in this place, he learned, but only Necropolis held such games. Brent didn't really know much about ancient Rome, but he supposed that he was getting an education now. The big question was, how do they know so much about the historical civilization to emulate it thus? Could this be some type of parallel development? He held no theory as to how this all got started, but there had to be an influence that brought this much detail. It all seemed very authentic.

The day came and somehow Brent knew that his number was up; he was going to have to go out there and kill someone with a sword that night. The crews came and set up the arena for the evening, and a guard came to his cell door and told him to stand ready.

"I'll never be ready, buddy," Brent said.

The guard made a funny noise, as if he'd bitten into something bitter. "If you are a coward, it is permitted that you may forfeit your life to honour Saturn. I will help steady you if you are afraid."

Brent was surprised by the guard's words. "I'm not a coward. I can kill if I have to. I just don't like it." He had seen death in the so-called "civilized" Sol System in the twenty-sixth century; while billions worked and lived a peaceful life, he made his way on the fringes of the law. Violence happened in his world, but no one was running around with a sword.

The guard took him out of his cell and into another room. The master of the arena, a bald, one-eyed man who was very tall and had a shitty disposition, met them there, and Brent was given a real sword and some minimal armour. A loose vest of light chain mail. A bronze wrist band for his sword arm. That was all except for his sword; two sided, lighter than he expected and sharp as death.

"How about a helmet?" Brent asked seriously.

"Bah!" The one eyed man spat. "No helmet for such as you."

Outsiders, would-be invaders; thats how they see us. *And they knew we were coming, at least after the big vessel grabbed us,* he thought. *Saturn sent out his little greeting party. This guy has got some kind of tech. He might not understand it himself, but he knew we had docked somehow.* Brent cursed himself for finally starting to reason out this madness at the worst possible time. The guard led him up to the gates, where he would make his entrance into the arena.

"Wait till I give the word," the guard said. The sound of heavy chains began and the gate lifted. Outside, the crowd cheered loudly.

"Blessings upon the children of Saturn!" Saturn stood tall at his balcony. "Another invader is in the arena tonight—wasn't the other one full of surprises? Maybe, if he survives, we will put the two in against each other!"

A huge cheer from the crowd.

"And here he comes!"

The guard gave Brent a shove, and he staggered out into the suddenly blinding light of the arena. Dust from the floor floated up in the hazy, humid air, making it hard to see the crowd or the details of his surroundings. Brass instruments blasted the air suddenly, and the crowd cheered as the far gate opened. Brent merely stood in his spot, holding his sword.

"And how could we forget Alexo the Bone Cutter!" Saturn introduced Brent's opponent.

Brent looked at the man; he was about the same height as Brent, but the man had a fair bit of weight on him. He was bald and had a face like a bulldog. Two leather straps crossed his torso, as did scars from a hundred wounds. On his left side, he carried a shield and on the right, a very wicked-looking sword; the blade was long and sharp on one side and oddly serrated on the other. *The damn thing could double as a saw*, Brent thought darkly. He was doing his best not to consider how Alexo got the title "Bone Cutter."

Brent was terrified. What civilized man would not be? He was clearly staring down a killer. Then he remembered that he'd taken two lives over the course of time himself, once when he was younger and still involved with outlaw gangs and once three years ago outside a dive bar at Io Station. Brent could kill in self-defence. He knew this, and that thought gave him courage as he and Alexo paced around each other.

The situation was grim, to say the least, and Brent was acutely aware of the fact.

He suddenly had an idea and went into action, pretending to be frightened out of his wits and backing up, away from Alexo. He stumbled and fell *intentionally*. With his shield hand, he scooped up some loose dirt from the arena floor.

Alexo came in fast, trying to take advantage of the fall. The Bone Cutter gripped his blade with both hands and swung down as if to chop Brent in half.

But Brent rolled to his left and came up fast, throwing the loose dirt into Alexo's eyes. Brent knew he had to be fast. He might not get another chance like this.

Alexo howled and clawed at his stinging eyes as he straightened up.

Brent rolled again and slashed his sword across the back of both of Alexo's legs.

It had worked for Helen, and it worked for him; a quick, dirty trick. As Alexo went down, Brent jumped forward and sunk his sword firmly into the man's guts.

Blood flowed. Alexo screamed once as he thrashed around on the ground.

Brent pulled his sword free. It was over.

The crowd had fallen quiet as this happened, but now some booed and others chattered in low voices.

"Guards! Seize him! Dishonourable little gnat who cheats. You will receive a coward's death!" Saturn screamed from his seat.

Men rushed out from all directions and surrounded Brent.

Brent merely dropped his sword and shield and raised his hands.

Two of the guards came and shackled Brent while the others watched. They led him back into the barracks underneath the arena. He was silent as they walked down steps and turned down a shadowy tunnel. The guards were abusive and mean now that Saturn had labelled him a cheater.

Suddenly to his great surprise, laser fire flashed out in the dim passage. One guard fell with a hole burnt through his armour. Before Brent could react, the other guard was snatched from behind with a grunt.

Two men stepped from the shadows and came toward him. They were not dressed in the Roman style, like the people in most of the city. They were outsiders.

Still rattled from the fight, Brent instinctively assumed a defensive position.

The two men stood still, then looked at each other.

"We're trying to rescue you, you fool," said one.

"Who the hell are you?" Brent said, finally grasping the fact that these were not Saturn's people.

"Your new best friends," said the taller man.

"I am Denzeel," said the shorter, darker-skinned man. "And this is the Tyrr of the Freemen. We must go now, or we will all die tonight."

"Wait, there were others with me. We were taken prisoner. I can't just leave them!" Brent said franticly.

"We know," Denzeel said quickly, while trying to hurry Brent along. "We have the woman and are trying to get the other man." He gestured to an opening in the floor of the room that they were approaching. "Now, hurry!"

Brent followed. It was the best option by a large margin, so he descended into the catacombs beneath the city of Augustine. His destiny, for the moment, was in the hands of the two unknown men leading him out of peril. Anything was better than the predicament that he'd been in.

7

REVELATIONS

HENDRICKS WAS FEELING better than he had in years, and he wasn't sure why. Was it the adrenalin rush of having successfully pulled off a rescue mission? Well, semi-successfully; there was the issue of the other stranger and, of course, the loss of Marcos. He had more than likely been slain while he attempted to rescue the third member of Brent's party. Was it the excitement of meeting someone from the Sol System after all this time? Or was it the dim hope given him by the fact that another vessel had wandered into the dark rift? Hope that one day he would be able to leave this world, the only world he had known for many years now.

They kept a dark camp now, Hendricks, Denzeel, Brent, and Helen. In a half-day, they'd made their way through Augustine's catacombs to a secret passage that led outside of the city limits. They hid among some dark hills about a kilometre southwest of Augustine. If their luck held, they'd be able to acquire horses the next day. The newcomers kept trying to ask a hundred questions, not a few about their companion, Simon.

Hendricks had explained that they had come as three to rescue three and had each been responsible for freeing one person. Denzeel went for Helen, Hendricks for Brent, and Marcos was to retrieve Simon. Something had gone wrong for Marcos, and he didn't show at the designated place. The ultimate fates of Marcos and Simon were unknown, although Hendricks held out little hope they were alive.

"Marcellus ... that is, Saturn ... is going to be pissed when he figures out what happened. When he realizes who it was that came into his city and stole his prize from him, he will respond somehow," Hendricks said, looking over at Denzeel. Denzeel nodded at the mention of Saturn's potential reprisal.

Helen, who had been fairly quiet up until then, spoke up with vehemence. "They're fucking pigs! Savages. Bloody slobbering primitives. What in the name of God is going on here? What happened here?"

"And you," Brent broke in. "You are not from this place. You came from outside, like us. What the hell is going on here?

"Okay, listen up," Hendricks said in an authoritative tone. "We are in no position for me to sit here and explain this whole mess to you. For the moment, try to understand that I got here essentially the same way that you did. Dark rift in space, time warp, and you got picked up by the *Crimson Star*'s AI. That's the name of this world ship. The lands inside the habitat are called Terraroma and, yeah, it's a lot like ancient Rome."

"Time warp?" Helen said nervously.

"That's right," Hendricks said. "To get here, you must have come through the rift. What year was it before you came here?"

"2567." Helen answered.

"Oh, God, that's weird," Hendricks said. "You must have been caught in the rift before Jones and I were, and yet I've been here for five years. You just arrived a short time ago. Time is strange here. The best I can figure is we are seven centuries or so from where we started."

"No, no, no. I'm not accepting any such goddamn thing. Are you trying to say that if we could manage to get out of here and back to the system, we'd be seven hundred years out of date?" Brent said, sounding exasperated as his voice began to rise.

"Keep your voice down!" Denzeel hissed at Brent. Hendricks came over closer to where Brent was sitting and squatted down to talk to him.

"Listen," Hendricks said. "I can imagine how pissed off and tired you folks must be. I'm sorry about your friend Simon. I lost a good man trying to get him out, and I don't know what else I can say, but you have got to get your shit together in here fast. This is a very dangerous world, and we're trying to help you.

"You have to trust me when I tell you I'll explain things to you when we are safe. Right now, we have to concentrate on getting away from this area. It is a long way to the Zingaris' camps." He paused for a moment, thinking, and then continued. "As for what I tell you, I don't really give a shit what you want to believe, but I'm giving the facts as I understand them. The sooner you accept some of these things, the better off you'll be."

That put any formal conversation to rest for the rest of the camp. The sun line had long since moved far away, and all was dark except for the few holographic stars that could be seen through the overcast of very real clouds. Rain was fine by Hendricks if it happened tonight; it helped create cover for their small group of travellers. Tomorrow, there was a village east of their position where he was certain they could acquire horses for the journey home. The infiltration of the arena complex was a job that had required great stealth, so they'd abandoned their horses when they'd arrived.

The mission had two purposes. One was to rescue the people from the recently boarded vessel. The other was to do some recon on the city of Augustine and on General Marcellus/Saturn.

What Hendricks had seen in Augustine was that the city had become decadent and cruel, with little support for the poor and sick. It amazed him how he'd fought side by side with Marcellus to liberate Augustine from Magnus Jupiter. They had destroyed the Magnus Jupiter avatar that had ruled these lands for centuries because it had become evil and corrupted. Corrupted by Loki, the thing from the dark rift. Within months of taking the city, Marcellus seemed to have gone mad and began conquering and killing any who opposed him. He went from liberator to tyrant in the blink of an eye. Another interesting fact they had discovered on this mission was that the locals no longer called their city "Augustine". The name they heard it called most often now was "Necropolis".

Now Hendricks has learned that it is believed Loki has survived and has somehow bent Marcellus to his will. Although he, himself, had seen no direct evidence of this, it was the belief among many that this was, in fact, the old evil risen again. The spirit of Magnus Jupiter, of Olympias, of the thing he called Loki. It had been purged from the system, but it did not die; perhaps it couldn't die, as Hendricks understood the concept.

Rain came and they moved on at dawn under Hendricks's instructions; a rainy day in Terraroma was a pretty dark day. The sunlight equivalency given off by the sun line would have been like a spring day in the northwest of North America on Earth. But it was, in reality, of course, much cooler than the real sun over Earth. The light spectrum given off by the sun line were no match for the cloud cover and the day was dark and gloomy. It did nothing for Brent and Helen's mood, but to Hendricks, it seemed to lighten his mood. He knew that as they moved into the nearby village, the reduced visibility would make them hard to spot. Denzeel was quiet and sullen, as had been his way for many years now.

Hendricks thought of the circumstances which had befallen Denzeel since Hendricks had arrived in Terraroma. After the first siege of Miceen, Hendricks had gone and stayed with Denzeel's family for a short time. Denzeel was at his happiest then.

When the revolutions—the uprisings against the "gods"—had begun, it put a terrible strain on Denzeel's relationship with his wife, Laurenna. She had wanted Denzeel to retire from being a soldier, but that wasn't going to happen when such a pivotal point in their history was at hand. So, Denzeel had ridden with Marcellus and Hendricks as they marched on Augustine five years ago. Civil war broke out at home while Denzeel was away, and that had cost them the life of their son, Bendel, as he followed his father's footsteps and became a soldier. That was enough for Laurenna, who left Denzeel at that point. There was no divorce as there was in Sol System culture; but the couple no longer lived together. Their marriage would only be finished if one or both chose new partners, or one of them died.

So Denzeel had followed Hendricks when he decided to leave Miceen and find a new life for himself in Terraroma. There had been no way back home that Hendricks could see, and he was happy to have a friend at such a despairing time. Together they had begun to rally some of the small nomadic tribes that had travelled the lands near the outskirts of the Great Desert. In time, Hendricks came to be sole leader of a large travelling people known as the Zingaris. This work created a third military force in Terraroma. The desert people were exceptional riders, and their archery skills were unmatched.

At the village, a small farming community called Crossroad, they were able to acquire provisions and horses for the long journey back to the rendezvous with the Zingaris. They had three horses—one to carry the provisions and two to carry the four of them. Helen rode behind Denzeel and Brent behind Hendricks. They did not stay in Crossroad long. As they departed, Hendricks could not help grinning as he watched Brent and Helen climb onto a horse for the first time. He recalled his own first awkward attempts to gain some skill in riding. He also remembered saddle sores and wondered if either of the two had even heard of them. *Well*, he surmised, *if they're going to survive in here, they've got a lot more than saddle sores to worry about.*

8

THE SOUL OF MICEEN

THE GOOD GODDESS herself held the residence within the structure that had once been known as the temple of Olympias. The woman who was the goddess was a mix of the human being who been Macy Jones and an artificially created avatar. Jones had been severely wounded when she battled the Olympias avatar. Close to death, Jones had been saved by the powerful AI; she had crawled onto the biobed Olympias used to maintain itself, and the Good Goddess had been created. She was now and forever linked to *Crimson Star*'s AI matrix.

The temple was now more like a community centre than a place of worship. The Macy Jones part of the equation that was the Good Goddess had little or no use for religious formality, although she had come to understand that the culture of Miceen demanded it. She went along with it because it made the citizens happy. It turned out that they liked the idea of a single, all-powerful ruler ... just not one who was sadistic or vindictive. The people had to learn how to rule themselves and it was her intention to teach them; in that way, she was in perfect alignment with the AI's population re-education program. Perhaps, in a generation, the people would be more confident to control their own destiny.

The Good Goddess sighed. *Why does history take such a long, long time?* forgetting, as she did, though, that every thought that she had was heard by the rest of the collective "brain" that she was now a part of.

A quick download of thoughts and theories of the humanity's slow crawl up out of the muck of time, until it actually began to warp its own evolutionary path.

Enough! she told herself. She considered the tasks at hand. There would be a meeting of people who work for the public interest today. Her first job, when she had become ruler of Miceen, was to abolish many of the old customs and practices that she felt actually did more harm than good. It was a slow uphill climb, all right. Where in human history it had taken millennia for cultures and governments to evolve to where they were in the twenty-sixth century, the goal here was to do it in centuries.

To say that she was not wholly herself would have been accurate in some interesting ways, and false in others. For example, Macy Jones had had an accurate sense of self both before and after her battle with Olympias/Loki. But she was not the same as before, perhaps because she had accepted that it was her fate and destiny to be where she was today. She felt a responsibility to this little world so strangely lost in time and space. Her physical body had been irreparably damaged in the battle with the Olympias avatar, and when she drove Loki out and merged with the AI system, a new body had been designed after her old one. A Jones avatar had been created, but her true consciousness was awash in the matrix with the two other components of the world mind.

Her physical appearance was striking; six feet tall with long, powerful legs and shining golden skin. Her hair was sleek black, in braids that hung to her shoulders. In fact, she looked more like an ancient Egyptian than a Roman.

She was happy to busy herself with the business of running the city state of Miceen, as well as introduce some new ideas to the overtly Roman society. For the duration of the morning, she did practical planning work with intelligent men and women who were dedicated to improving life in Miceen. This always made her feel human again, although she wasn't sure if she really fit the definition anymore. Instant access to all the data stored in the Magnus 9 AI system, plus all of Commander Vokova's memories and information, was an irresistible tool when she was doing this work. The biggest problem with her ambition to raise the population up was all the damage that Loki did to this culture, having perpetuated civil wars for centuries. It couldn't just be wiped all away in a few years.

The Good Goddess sighed once again, and this time the hard-working citizens who laboured with her picked up on their goddess's *boredom* or frustration. They only knew that her thoughts were straying elsewhere. Jones was sorry that this was so, but she was dreading her next duties of the day. Some of the people from her inner circle knew that today, following the rites of Minerva, the Good Goddess was going to address the people of Miceen. It was an address Jones had dreaded ever having to make, but one that was now unavoidable. Miceen was under threat, and the population had to be prepared.

After she had completed the day's work with her advisers and such, she retired to her own private chambers to prepare herself for the evening's ceremony. She looked into the full-length mirror, which was actually highly polished silver, and felt very strange. She was not the woman she had always known, but then, again, she was also not the frightening avatar that Olympias had been. She was something else again.

When she had fought the creature Loki, he had been inhabiting the Olympias avatar at that time. Macy Jones had been gravely wounded during the battle and had merged with the very computer systems that were running all of Terraroma. Half by accident and half by the help of Commander Vokova, Jones had survived inside the collective mind while her body was repaired and modified in the same manner that constructed the physical avatars of Magnus Jupiter and Olympias. She was now nearly a whole foot taller than she had been, and there were other changes also. Her skin, which had been a light brown, was now a dark, shiny gold. The eyes were the worst—two jet-black orbs with pinprick red pupils. Unearthly looking was the net result.

Vokova was there in her mind now, telling her again about the rites of Minerva. He would make sure she got all the words right. Jones told him to leave it alone when she addressed the people gathered. It would be a large crowd because they all knew the Good Goddess had something to say to them tonight.

When the time came, the ritual was performed with little or no modifications since someone had dreamed it up in the ancient world of Earth over 5,000 years ago. Jones was loath to admit it, but the ritual relaxed her. Now it was time to spill the beans to the hundreds of citizens who were gathered.

She stood before the assembly and raised her arms, asking for silence. The crowd complied. She felt a physical weariness and knew that she would soon have to replenish her avatar form. This was the darkest downside of the avatar to Jones; she had to absorb other biomatter, on occasion, to survive inside the avatar. She was a great deal more selective about where the biomatter came from. *That's enough of that for now*, she told herself and turned to the task at hand.

"Good people of Miceen, blessings abound. Tonight, I must sadly share sour tidings with you. General Marcellus, who was born and raised in this city, who has become the dictator of Augustine is now, sadly, fully possessed by the old, ancient evil. The evil has gone by many different names—Magnus Jupiter, Olympias, Loki—and now I understand that it utterly possesses Marcellus and calls itself Marcellus Saturanius Maximus, or merely Saturn! I have told you that this is an evil from outside, from the darkest shadows of space.

"Now, Marcellus is and was our brother and he is not wholly responsible for what is happening. However, I know the general, and I know his ambitious nature. He has been a fool, but he is paying too high a price for his mistakes."

A rustle of voices ran through the assembly of citizens. They understood the implication of these words.

Jones kicked herself for beating around the bush and decided to get down to the hard part. "Good people of Miceen, our peace and our way of life are threatened. I am loath to speak these words to you, but we must prepare for war! We felt safe to disband the army three years ago, but now we must build up our defences lest we are caught by sudden aggression. I believe that it is coming. We must be prepared. Conscriptions will begin in one week. Anyone with officer experience may volunteer for a commission anytime before that.

"Please understand that I would not call for war if there was any other way. We are peaceful people, but even a good and peaceful city must protect itself. It is important that you understand the difference between the coming war and all the other conflicts the good people of Miceen have had to endure over the years past. We fight to protect our new way of life; we fight for freedom!"

These words were met with a loud cheer. A good sign.

"Now, go home to your families and remember that it is the family and our way of life that we are protecting. Love your friends and family and have no fear; we are not descendants of fearful men. We will do what we must. A Great Council is called to gather the forces of all free people in Terraroma. Your chosen representatives will give you information as it comes in.

"Blessings abound, good people of Miceen. Good night."

Jones, the Good Goddess, moved away from the assembly. When she was alone, she noted her new body didn't shed tears. Her soul, however—the essence of who she was—burnt with sadness. *Better to get these emotions over with.* It was time to summon the warrior within her.

9
SAFE HAVEN

BRENT WAS TIRED, frustrated, somewhat confused, and worst of all, his entire crotch was in agony from riding on the damned horse. He was getting the hang of it, though, doing a lot better on the second day compared to the first. He knew that Denzeel was keeping an eye on him. He wasn't quite sure what to make of Denzeel, who was a fairly small man but seemed to be made of iron sinews and had the reflexes of a cat. When Denzeel spoke to him now, it was always in a respectable and patient tone. He liked this strange man. Hendricks, on the other hand, was the kind of man that Brent had known all his life; a vagabond, a hustler, and most importantly, a person from the same Sol System culture as he and Helen. Who Hendricks was here in this world, he wasn't certain yet. A leader of some kind; that much was obvious.

The most startling revelation yet was that Brent was convinced he had actually heard of Hendricks, once upon a time back there in the system. But what was all that crazy shit about time that he was talking about? Some explanation had better be coming soon, or he didn't know what he would do. This feeling was compounded by the fact that he didn't even know what he could do under the circumstances. Well, this was still a big improvement from Augustine and that madman Saturn.

It was at this time, riding high in a saddle without immediate concern for his life, that Brent really got a good look at the incredible panorama that Terraroma had to offer. He looked at the horizon, or at least where his eyes told him it should be. But the horizon was not really to be found. His eyes climbed up into the sky, and he saw the lands that were off in a distant part of the cylinder. To the far southeast, Brent could see a massive body of water, a small ocean or a large inland sea. The strangest part was that he was he was looking *upward* at distant places through the light cloud cover that hung in the centre of the great cylinder.

"Pretty damn impressive, isn't it?" said Helen, who had been watching him study the world around him. She looked pretty good, in spite of the things they'd been through in the last few days. He remembered how well she had handled herself in the area.

"Yes, it is," he said. "You were something back in the arena. You've got a few more skills than you advertised when I hired you for the job we were on."

"I like to think that I'm a realist, Mr. Brent. We are not really different from the people here. We do whatever we have to do in order to survive. We are still half savage, and I have always kept that in mind on every job I've ever worked. The rules and tactics are different out in the system, but all comes down the same. Expect the unexpected."

"Well, it's pretty damned easy to get killed in here. And hey, you can drop the 'Mr. Brent.' Just Jim or Brent will do."

"Okay," Helen responded and motioned toward Hendricks, who was listening to them. He came up and positioned himself so that he could speak to both of the two newcomers.

"We have made some good distance now, and these are safe lands. We will meet with my Zingaris by tomorrow. This might be a good time to answer some of your questions," Hendricks said, looking back and forth between them.

As they rode along at a relaxed pace, Hendricks told them his entire story from the day he and Jones had escaped from the doomed *Calypso*. He explained in as much detail as he could what had happened to the *Crimson Star* and how this whole upside-down world had gotten started. He spoke of the collective AI and how Jones had sacrificed herself while driving the alien entity from the rift out of the AI system. To maintain the working balance of the system and to maintain its new protocols, Jones allowed her essence, her mind, to merge with the AI collective.

Finally, he spoke of how the alien entity hadn't been destroyed, only purged from the system, and how they believed that the threat remained inside Marcellus.

"Well, he's pretty damn big and very weird when I spoke to him," Brent said.

"You spoke to him?" Hendricks exclaimed. "He didn't just throw you in the arena?"

"Oh, yeah, he had me up in his throne room. Asked me to help him out, although I have no idea how I was going to do that."

Hendricks had Brent repeat the story in as much detail as he could recall. Finally, he seemed satisfied and stopped questioning Brent.

"There is to be a special war council in the near future. All the free peoples of Terraroma will be there. You will be required to attend," Hendricks said quietly and smiled. Then he rode on ahead.

As he moved away, Helen found that she liked Hendricks very much. He was a man by her idea of what a man should be; straightforward and honest. She knew Brent mentioned that he'd heard of this guy back in the system. He said that Hendricks was a well-know player around the system. He had been involved with a gang when he was a youth, but became a lone wolf after that. Helen knew that Brent didn't trust Hendricks completely. She could see that he was a big wheel on this little world even before they reached his people. He was a natural leader. She couldn't help but like him, and she wondered what he thought of her. Well, enough of that for now. They continued to ride.

※ ※ ※

They soon met the Zingaris, and Brent was surprised how much they resembled the nomadic peoples on horseback from Earth's ancient history. To his surprise, there were many camels, covered wagons, and every manner of travelling apparatus one could think of. Entire extended families were living in this moving city; women and children coming and going as they would on market day. Brent observed that the gender roles were different here, nothing like they would have been to the nomadic Arab tribes on the ancient Sahara.

Both Denzeel and Hendricks had spoken to them about the Zingaris. The nomadic folk were divided into houses which were named and loosely modelled after the ancient zodiac from Europe on Earth. Hendricks was revered as the Tyrr, and when they arrived at this roaming, caravan many people approached him with a half bow, awaiting orders. Hendrick gave out those orders in a friendly tone.

Helen seemed somewhat less than impressed by the desert nomads. "Well, I guess that we're going to have to join the circus," she said as they were directed toward one of many tents that had been set up before their arrival. Hendricks had directed Denzeel to see to their new guests' comfort. They were given a single tent for both of them, and when Helen objected to the idea of sleeping under the same tent as Brent, Denzeel held up a hand with a confused expression on his face and said, "Tonight, we have two extra mouths to feed; the least that you could do is share one tent."

That was the end of that. Helen felt a bit foolish and was pleased to find a divider that ran the length of their tent. She had never felt uncomfortable around Brent on the shuttle before, so why would she feel that way now? Once they settled in, she was amazed at how comfortable it was; a beautiful rug was laid out over other layers of rug, and the tent itself was designed to allow airflow if desired. After being served a great meal of recipes neither of them had ever heard of before, she spoke with Brent before they went to sleep.

"Do you trust this guy, Brent?" she asked.

"I'd heard of him out in the system, a drifter and a grifter both. He used to run with some rebel group when he was a kid. I heard he can rebuild the drive in a class 2 shuttle in his sleep. I don't know what to think about what he said about being trapped here.

"Trust him? Seems to me that he's a pretty important person around here, judging from that army he's got out there. He seems kinda strange, I think, like his mind is far away at times," Brent said. "One of those deep-thinking types."

"Well, that's kind of a nice quality in someone," Helen said with a small smile. "You don't see it a lot anymore." She kept her new feeling about Hendricks to herself and wondered if Brent was picking up on them.

10
WHEN IN ROME

THERE WAS VERY little light in the part of the dungeon that Simon was imprisoned in, but his eyes were very well adapted to the gloom. He had lost track of time and really didn't know how long he had been locked away down here. It was a truly horrible place, where rats gnawed at the bones of deceased prisoners, and the stench was enough to make a civilized man choke. A tiny light a hundred yards away was all he got to know about the passing of time down in this hell hole.

Two days ago, Simon had heard someone being tortured in another part of the dungeon. The sound of the screams, which grew more high-pitched and horrible as time went on, no longer seemed to bother him as they had at first. He sat in his cell and protectively cradled the arm with the missing hand.

He was in hell, he figured. Simon had stopped talking on the day he was captured; he kept recalling the sight of Brent cauterizing the stump where his hand used to be, and he could not forget the smell of his own burnt flesh. He knew that Brent had probably saved his life when he did that. Simon couldn't help but hate the man anyway. *He* had brought them here. *He* had taken them all to hell. Simon relished the idea of enacting revenge upon Brent.

Simon's mind was dark now, and it swam with dark thoughts. He had changed, he knew, and he was changing still. It was bad enough to be maimed and imprisoned in this hellhole, but some time ago, he had become aware of a presence invading his mind. His memory contained blank spots and a dreamlike memory of flying through the darkness. The presence was both repulsive and inviting at the same time. He struggled to hold onto the world that he had known.

- *Just surrender, and it will all work out.* -

The words kept echoing in his fevered mind. His will grew weaker and weaker.

Eventually, guards came and savagely dragged him from his cell within the dungeon. Much time had passed, and the sudden re-emergence into normal daylight stung his eyes and temporarily blinded him. As they shoved him along, he began to adapt to being outside of the dungeon, and this change began to give him hope that he would survive this experience. The leg shackles the guards had put on him clanked on the palace floor when he entered, and the sound echoed in the cavern-like structure.

They brought him before the large wooden doors of the room, which was his destination.

"Enter," said one guard, who opened the doors. The other pushed him inside, and the doors were closed behind him. Apparently, the soldiers were not going to come in with him. The room had a musty smell, and the light was dim. Weak torches sputtered at the far end.

"Hello, Simon. It's good to meet you in person at last."

As the voice spoke to him from the far end of the room, the torches picked up and illuminated the chamber. A man sat on an oversized, broken marble throne. The man was large and muscular. By the length of his limbs, Simon could see that he was taller than most of the people he had seen in this world thus far. The man stood slowly and stretched. Simon's thought was confirmed; he was at least six foot three, to use the common form, easily a few inches taller than Simon. The man walked toward Simon and gestured to come into the room.

Simon came forward, dragging his leg restraints and extended his good hand in greeting.

"I am Saturn," said the man, ignoring the offered hand. He looked down at Simons leg shackles and frowned.

"Is that any way to treat a guest?" Saturn said. He bent down quickly and, to Simon's surprise, broke off the left shackle with two powerful hands. "There are a hammer and chisel on that table over there. You can do the rest." He gestured off to the side of the room.

"But I only have one hand," Simon said, feeling pathetic.

"Let's see how smart you are," Saturn replied with an ugly smile.

Simon went over to the table and tried to find a way to use the hammer and chisel to remove the other shackle. He struggled with it for a time, dropped both instruments several times.

I'll be damned if I'm going to give up, he thought. He could feel Saturn's eyes on him as he worked and suddenly realized that he was having the same sensation now as in the dungeon when his mind was invaded. He looked up at Saturn suddenly.

"Yes, Simon, that was me getting familiar with the little meat pack behind your eyes," Saturn said. He bent again and tore the right shackle from Simon's leg as if it were made of paper. "Saturn is merciful to his friends and deadly to his enemies. Today we must decide which of those categories you fall in to.

"This is my world, Simon, and I am its god. This is a troubled world, and order must be restored to it. To do this, I wish to gather those who are faithful to assist and, in doing so, gather glory for themselves and the greater glory of Saturn."

Simon looked down at the place where the shackle was. He suddenly felt good and felt a strange gratitude to this man who was obviously more than just a man. Simon had always had a unique instinct to follow the winner, and he was prepared to go along with Saturn. At first, when he was brought to the room, he was willing to cooperate with whoever if it kept him out of the dungeon. Now he was thinking, *It makes real sense to follow this man who is more than a man.* Simon could sense the power that emanated from Saturn.

"Help me, and I will help you, Simon. In the world you came from, could they replace your lost hand?" Saturn asked him.

"If they had lost a limb, they might be able to reattach it," Simon said. "There would be the option of getting a bionic hand, or, if someone wanted to try and take the time, there is a new procedure to grow a new hand."

Saturn then gestured to another corner of the chamber where the damaged medical biobed was stored.

Simon saw what looked like an antique emergency medical bay. which had been modified in some unique ways; he walked over and examined the bed. The power source was intact, but the interface was damaged. After a few minutes, he came to the conclusion that it could be repaired. If the right materials were available, it might be possible to get it working.

The equipment had been modified using some type of tech that he didn't understand. He thought that it was possible that some alien tech was applied to this machine. Simon noticed that close by was a shallow, empty pool like an inset hot tub. The shape was all wrong, though, so it certainly wasn't a hot tub. This was highly unusual, and he couldn't think of what purpose it might have held.

"I think that I could help with this. I don't know if we have what it takes to repair it in way of materials, but the basic concept is an old one." Simon spoke slowly and carefully. "I believe we could fix this."

"Then I think that we shall be friends, Simon," Saturn said with a big smile, and he spread his arms wide and laughed aloud. Then he came over to Simon and broke off the remaining shackles off. "Your friends, the people you came here with, have refused my friendship."

"Well, that was bloody stupid," Simon said.

"So, it comes time to make a choice, Simon. If we are to be friends, you will be a guest in my city. If you are going to be rude like your companions ... well, then I guess it's back to the dungeon," Saturn said to him, bloodshot eyes seeming to glow in the dark gloom of this corner of the throne room.

Simon could not meet this man's eyes, so he bowed his head instead. "I would like to be your friend. Maybe I could help out with some things around here." As he spoke, Simon began to feel better; the anger and resentment in his heart were transforming into a dark joy. This was the path to take.

"Swear your allegiance to me, Simon, and you will be set free."

"I swear," Simon said. Now he felt right; he straightened his back and looked over at the one called Saturn; Tall, powerful, and possessed of a face that looked dead in repose but evil when animated. Some alien presence made the man emanate power. A throbbing expression of emotion. An electric pulse.

Simon had found a new home, although he didn't know it at that moment. Saturn set him free within the palace and supplied him with a place to live. He had good food and was given whatever luxury was available. Women came to him on occasion, and Simon was as snug as a bug in a rug when he fell off to sleep most nights. He worked on repairing Saturn's machine, and as long as he was making progress, his life became one of comfort and leisure. He learned all about Terraroma, Saturn, and the history of the people, but he heard it from the perspective of Saturn; Simon never heard about the years when Saturn was called Marcellus and, as a matter of fact, before long, he could think of Saturn as nothing less than a saviour.

11
THE COMING OF THE AUXCONITES

HENDRICKS WAS SITTING alone in his tent and considering the recent news that had been imparted on him. The alien that Vokova had called Loki was alive and had taken possession of Marcellus, this much was beyond debate, and he was fully intent on conquering all the lands of Terraroma. *What had become of Marcellus?* he wondered. *Is he trapped inside of his body but unable to act because of Loki? Or was he discarded, kicked out of his own body like an unwanted passenger?* It was kind of a moot point because the thing *had* to be destroyed once and for all. This was probably the human race's first contact with an alien intelligence, and it wasn't turning out too well. He thought of the possibility of an entire race of creatures like Loki and he shuddered. *Could the thing be something else? A one-off? A mutant? There's probably no way to find out.* He sighed heavily.

Hendricks was considering the problem of his newly arrived friends. These people were from home, from the system like him, and close enough to the same time so as not to make a difference. They were players, just like him. Of this, he was sure. He wondered if Brent would confess what job they were on. Professional smugglers, the man was anyway. The woman, Helen, he wasn't so sure about. She seemed out of place somehow next to Brent, who Hendricks had no doubt he'd heard of along back channels where one might acquire illegal gear. He had no idea how they fit into this crazy place, if they would adapt and survive, or what would happen.

He was just coming to the next in his list of concerns, the upcoming "council of free people," when he heard a great clamour and the sound of anxious voices calling around the camp. He knew his Zingaris well enough to know that if it sounded like this, then something was up. The Zingaris were not known to frighten easily.

He was up and out the door of his tent when Denzeel came running up to him; Denzeel's face also showed great concern as he approached.

"Tyrr!" he cried. "We have an army assembled off our western flank! They came from nowhere!"

Hendricks stared at his friend. *What the hell is he talking about? Assembled off our flank? He did not say "attacks." How can an army sneak up on a camp the size of a small city?* Hendricks ran in the direction of the disturbance, Denzeel with him. All around him, men and women were arming themselves, for they all knew the drill if the camp was under attack. Up ahead, his people had set up a defence perimeter, and then finally, when he got closer, he could see what the alarm was about.

There, with their weapons shining in the late daylight, were row upon row of fierce-looking foot soldiers. They stood at attention, at the ready, with spears, pikes, long swords, and axes. A few others—tall, unarmed men, officers perhaps—were marching back and forth in front of the assembled soldiers. It was an odd scene, to be sure. He spoke to the person on watch, who claimed that they were just there. Nothing there one minute, and then he turned around, and there they were! Just as they are now, Hendricks was told.

"I'll go out," Denzeel said, and he set off toward the besieged flank. A few moments later, he was striding out toward the tall men in the front of the army. Seeing him approach, one of the men came toward him. He was unarmed, as was Denzeel. The two men stopped 20 feet apart from one another. Hendricks, who watched from a distance, thought this was one of the strangest scenes he'd witnessed in a while, and in Terraroma, that was saying something.

* * *

"Do you speak for these people?" the tall man asked Denzeel.

"I'm not the leader, but I speak with his authority. Who are you and what do you want? Why do you move this aggression against a peaceful encampment?" Denzeel responded.

"Aggression? No aggression has been made! We are peaceful people with honest intentions who wish to parlay with your leader."

Denzeel stood still and was silent. This went on for a few moments until the man finally continued.

"I am Oniman. We are the Auxconites, the people who inhabit the outer realms of this world. We have known of the other peoples of this world, but we chose to remain hidden for reasons of our own. The time has come to fulfill the prophecies, and we come out of the shadows at last. We must speak to your leader. There are many filters to be cleaned, and we should now speak together."

Denzeel was trying to come to a quick decision, and he knew that lives could depend on what he did now. The army on the western flank looked even deadlier up close; he doubted that the Zingaris could stand against it for long, if at all. His gut told him that the man, Oniman, was honest in his words. A slow trust, perhaps? He would try.

"We offer safe passage on our word for three people to enter our camp and parlay with the Tyrr," Denzeel said.

"Then we accept!" said Oniman.

"In one hour." Denzeel turned and walked back into the camp.

Hendricks paced around in his war tent; this was a very strange occurrence that he certainly hadn't anticipated. This was a mystery, these odd tall men, who said they were peaceful but had a massive army to back them up. He imagined that if they did wish to take the Zingaris, they could have done it by now.

Auxconites? Something was starting to make a strange sense about these visitors. Perhaps meeting with them would confirm his theory; this was a second separate culture that developed somewhere else on this ship. It was, after all, huge beyond belief. He would wait and see.

The meeting was to be three and three. Obviously, he'd take Denzeel as his second. He could have picked a dozen worthy warriors to sit in with him, but he had an idea. He sent Denzeel to get Mr. Brent. *Let's get a perspective from the outer system.*

After being brought to the war tent and told what was going on, Brent was understandably shocked; he'd only recently learned about the army parked on the west side.

"You want me to assess these new folks like I'm a zookeeper or something?" Brent said. He took two backward steps as if he were going to turn and leave the tent again. "I'm not interested in playing war in here with you guys. We want to get back home."

Hendricks suddenly realized how badly planned this gathering was. The timing was no good and that was his fault. He tried his best to be calm and centred, like a good leader. He spoke in an almost apologetic tone. He walked over closer to the newcomer so he could speak to him directly.

"Brent, I know I'm asking you to play catch-up pretty quick, but I need your help, and I know you're a capable man. You survived in here. Many wouldn't have—both of you really held it together in Necropolis.

"But you have to accept something—we're trapped here, outside normal space. Even if we had the power to get back, the time distortion would mean that you'd be a relic in a world that doesn't know you; we're hundreds of years ahead of where we started. That trader you said you came in on can't reach any kind of speed to beat the physics inside this space. Surely you must realize I'm telling you the truth? Don't you think that we wanted to get out before we came to understand that it wasn't going to happen?"

"I'm pretty good with an engine myself," Brent said and then adopted an expression of resignation. "Okay, I get what you're trying to say. But why get involved in the people here like this, all this Roman army and desert nomad stuff? Why bother?"

"I know you want to stay alive as much as anyone, Brent, and this is the way to do it. That crazy bastard Saturn isn't going to stay in Augustine – Necropolis, as he calls it, much longer, and this is something that'll kill us all. Now this other army shows up; I need help, and I'm asking you to pitch in. I want to know what you think of these people."

After a few minutes, Brent nodded his agreement, and it was almost time to sit down with these new people. Denzeel left the tent to go and escort Oniman and his companions to the war tent.

"There's going to be a big meeting coming up soon, with all the free people who oppose Saturn," Hendricks said as they waited. "I think that you and Helen should both be included in that. You've been up close and personal and lived to talk about it. I know that there are people who want to ask you questions."

"You people sure have a lot to talk about around here, huh?" Brent groaned.

Finally, the Auxconites arrived. Just like Oniman, the two companions who came with him were exceptionally tall, thin, and pale Caucasians. They wore loose clothing and were all bald, giving them the impression of monks. Hendricks couldn't help noticing that they seemed somehow different when he first saw them marching in front of their soldiers and yelling out orders.

All six of them sat around a circular table that was used for such occasions. Hendricks, Denzeel, and Brent on one side, and Oniman and his aides across from them. Oniman introduced the two others as Onyxi and Olivista.

By way of introduction, Hendricks began by looking straight at the man he knew to be Oniman, and said, "I am John Hendricks. I am also the Tyrr of the Zingaris, who roam the open lands like the wind. This man is Denzeel, and he is my most highly regarded, my number two, if you prefer. This other man is Brent, an associate from the worlds beyond."

This introduction surprised Brent, if not the Auxconites.

Oniman gave the closest thing to a smile that anyone had seen yet, then cleared his throat and began to speak. "In honesty, good people, we do owe you an explanation because we know what a surprise it must be to only learn of us now. We have always been here, since the first days of chaos and upheaval, and we have lived and grown to serve God and His Seed, in which we all live. We have always lived within the shell of this world, of God's Seed. For many years, we did not believe that anyone did or could live within the open habitat. We believed that the habitat was laid waste in the days of chaos. We lived and worked at the old professions as best we could until, one day, war broke out among us. A long, civil blood feud would describe it best. Much knowledge was lost, and much fell into disrepair during these wars, which lasted for a century, as we tell time. Finally, beyond all hope, we learned to make peace again. Since that time, we have been pacifists.

"It was not until the long peace came that we discovered that people were alive and whole cultures were living within the habitat. We hadn't thought it possible. When we saw what had become of the inhabitants of the habitat, we were shocked and saddened at the evil which had oppressed the people. I speak of Magnus Jupiter and Olympias.

"We began to move among you at times in order to learn what we could of these demon tyrants. All of our people share the gift of stealth; we can manoeuvre without being noticed, which is not the same as not being seen. We did not interfere with anything; we only observed. Until, one day, the demon slayers came to the Seed from the worlds beyond this world. We know that one is now known as the Good Goddess. We keep our distance from Miceen out of respect for the goddess."

Oniman then looked at Hendricks, and this time he did smile. "And so that leaves one other, and that is you, sir, the one who slew Magnus Jupiter. You are highly revered among our people, and we stand ready to assist you in the coming storm."

The speech had left Hendricks feeling a bit self-conscious, but he moved ahead as best he could. What a strange culture. What weird religion did they follow? Religion, even in the twenty-sixth century, remained a source of strife for the human race. The names might have changed, and there were some new beliefs, but people continued to maim and murder in the name of God. Who knew what else had developed after seven centuries?

"Uh, thank you, sir. Those are kind words indeed, but please understand that as Tyrr, I am responsible for the Zingaris, and I must state the obvious; you are here, speaking peace, while you command a large army right off our western flank. No one talks peace unless they are prepared to back it up with war, is that it?"

"I've told you how we are pacifists now and how we have developed new skills," Oniman continued. "We had to know that you were truly advocating peace. You still chose peace, even when threatened by a superior force. You have nothing to fear from us, and you may consider the army disbanded."

As Oniman said this, his two companions bowed their heads as if in prayer. Moments later, a great cry of astonishment was heard throughout the camp. A man hurriedly came to the tent and announced that the army had vanished.

Even as he looked at the messenger in confusion, Hendricks heard voices outside in the camp, astonishment in their talk. Clearly, there was something else going on here. Something weirder than he'd first imagined when he sat down with these odd emissaries from the outer shell of the *Crimson Star*.

"Explain these events to us, Oniman. How has a large and formidable army first snuck up on us and then disappeared?"

"Because it was never there. It was an illusion, a thought projection." Oniman said. "You see, we have no real weapons, and our numbers are small."

There are various looks from the men on the other side of the table; astonishment, anger, and incomprehension.

Oniman saw the confusion on their faces and explained that God had given them the power to project images into the minds of others. He went on to say that his two companions had projected the army; it was a technique that they called the physical repellant—working together, two or more Auxconites could project a large illusion to an entire group.

"We are no threat to you, but we recognize the threat in the north. Saturn, he is the same evil that was the other two. But he is still a man somehow, and we know that he was once General Marcellus of Miceen. We come to assist and respectfully wish a place at the meeting of free peoples. Yes, we know about even that."

Hendricks rested his chin on his fist and sat quietly looking at Oniman. He truly did not know what to make of the man or the incredible things that they were hearing and witnessing.

At his side, he could almost feel Denzeel bristling with anger; he was sure Denzeel thought this man was lying, and he resented being spied upon as Oniman described.

Hendricks, however, believed it. Why not? It certainly wasn't any crazier than anything else in Terraroma; AI's playing God, the glory of ancient Rome right in your own back yard. So why not the mutant offspring of the Auxiliary Control crews, living in the walls of the ship like rats. These strange men came with powerful psychic abilities. This was unbelievable, and it made them dangerous.

Hendricks looked over at Denzeel, and nodded to his friend.

"Oniman, do you understand that you're travelling aboard a world ship, lost outside of normal space time?" Hendricks asked his visitor.

Oniman looked a bit frustrated by the statement but maintained his cool composure as before. "I understand that we all have our purpose to play as we live within the Seed of God. God's Seed is on its way to the holy light. From that union, a new world will be born."

Hendricks was amazed how the Auxconites' mythology fits with the original purpose of the world ship. The *Crimson Star* was originally en route to Barnard's Star to found a new world for the human race. These people had maintained the original mandate within the dogma. How many centuries did they live in maintenance corridors and auxiliary control sections of the ship before they lost the true knowledge of the ship and its purpose?

Even now, strange as they were, they still had a better level of understanding of the real situation. Hendricks believed Oniman's story, but there was a hesitation in his gut. Hendricks had come to rely on Denzeel's counsel all these years, and he could already see that his friend was mistrustful of these new people. However, the more to stand against Saturn, the better.

"Yes, I believe that you should have a seat at the council. But I wish to know how the others feel about this. Brent, did you want to say something?" Hendricks asked.

Brent, who had been sitting and listening, was still trying to get his head around the illusionary army, or how it was even possible that this could be done. Holograms of some type? No way. Anyone would have sworn that they could see, hear, and even smell the army that was once on their flank. "Maybe it would be a good idea if one of you explained how you can do these 'thought projections.' With a power like that, how do we know when you are being honest with us? You've just demonstrated how easy it is to deceive us."

"I suppose that you will have to take us on our word," Oniman said.

That was enough for Denzeel. He stood quickly and spoke his mind. "First, you spy upon us and hide from us. Then you deceive us directly. And now you ask us to trust you? This is madness. Hendricks, the Tyrr knows that I will follow his lead and do as he commands. But I do not trust these strangers. Will you fight Saturn with your paper army?" Denzeel sat back down.

Hendricks was in a conundrum. He agreed with what the others were saying, but he didn't want to dismiss this mystery so soon. For the first time in many years, there came a new angle to the tale of the *Crimson Star*.

Maybe there was some kind of knowledge among the Auxconites that might help them escape from this madhouse in space? He knew this was wishful thinking, but he could also see how they could provide some tactical assistance against Saturn. He could use his power to override the others. As Tyrr, his was the final say in this camp.

Hendricks rose with a small sigh.

"Oniman, as you can see, there is a mixed reaction to your sudden appearance. The points that my friends have spoken of are legitimate causes for concern."

Onyxis, the companion to the left of Oniman, spoke suddenly and out of turn. "We truly believed that you would see us as allies once we—"

Oniman raised his hand and gestured for the man to be silent.

Hendricks nodded thanks to Oniman, and he continued. "Yes, we have concerns about you, but we would under any circumstance, anyway. Before I became their leader, the Zingaris taught me that in the desert, all a man has is his word. This began to show me a better way to live, and I adopted their culture as mine. You come to me and say to take you on your word. And so, I will, I will vouch for you at the Great Council, and you shall have a seat. You alone, Oniman. Come back to us as seven days pass, and I will tell you where and when the council meets."

12

FRIENDS AND FOES

AFTER PARTICIPATING IN the parlay between the Zingaris and the Auxconites, Brent went to search for Helen. In Brent's spinning mind, he still considered Helen to be the last voice of reason in this mad situation. She was a highly intelligent and straightforward person to have on a mission, and he valued her opinion. He could see her attraction to Hendricks and quickly dropped any thoughts he had about her. Still, they had landed in this strange place together, and it was high time they had a discussion about getting out of here, if that was still possible. He wasn't sure if he trusted Hendricks and his great tale about time warps and all that.

He found Helen deep in the Zingaris' camp, talking to some of the women from the House of the Lion. She saw him coming and wrapped up whatever the talk had been.

When she looked at Brent, he saw an expression on her face that he'd never seen before. Was it determination? No, something else. Then it hit him, and he was surprised. Helen looked happy, more relaxed than he had seen her before. That was saying a lot in this place.

"You look happier here. What's the secret?" Brent asked her.

"No secret," she said, "and I'm not sure that 'happy' is the word I'd use. Since we got away from that madman, well, this camp anyway just seems nicer than tracking com signals and chasing infection codes around in my brain. It's a simple life that they have here and to be honest, that seems nice after what we've been through."

"I think you and I should have a talk," Brent said. "We came into this situation together, and maybe we can get out of it together. This whole thing is crazy—everything since we got away from the peacekeeper, the soldiers like Romans, that city, the arena, and then that army outside—"

"Vanishes!" Helen injected. She was well aware of what was going on outside the camp and for a time, was certain that they'd gone from one bad situation into another one.

"Yeah. Hendricks had me stay in the room while he parlayed with the Auxconites, and…"

Helen's face went dark. "What? And I got left out like a good female…"

"Hey, I'm sure it wasn't like that." Brent answered.

"Hendricks, you asshole, you really disappoint me," Helen said, as if he were in the room.

"I'm 50/50 on the guy as it is. I thought that maybe we test some of these crazy things he's saying, like the idea that we can't get back—or if we did, we would be lost in time. Do you think we travelled through time as he said?" Brent said rapidly.

"I don't know," Helen said. "My wetware has been dead except for a bizarre single line of noise. I turned everything off as best I could. I could run a diagnostic on my wetware even without being in range of other tech. I don't use the tech in my head to it's full potential at all, but it has provided many employment opportunities, if you know what I mean."

"Of course. That's why I hired you," Brent said flatly. "Time can be strange. Everyone knows that, but this is about trying to get back. And I would really like to get back."

"Okay." Helen felt her neck muscles tighten. "Give me a bit of time. I'll try to run a diagnostic, as I said, and it'll establish a timeframe between now and when I was scanning the peacekeeper ship. That should hopefully give us something other than our perception of how much time has gone by. I'll come and find you when I have something to tell you."

Brent left then and went to get settled in the small tent that had been provided for them. Helen sat still and forced herself to slow down her breathing; she was apprehensive about doing this, partly because her wetware had never had to be shut down before and partly because of what she might learn from this experiment.

Her mind turned the wetware back on and the single thin sound that had been there before returned. All that noise told her was that if there was tech awake on the ship, it was either well-screened or beyond her wetware's ability to connect. She filtered out the sound.

Next, she tried to flip back to the initial scans that she took of the peacekeeper. If anyone had been watching her at that moment, they would have seen her blinking her eyes repeatedly and making odd gestures in her line of vision. What she saw, however, was a translucent interpretation of memory "files." Every single thing that she had done since the day the wetware was installed was saved in her augmented mind, so in theory, it should be right there. But it wasn't.

Events in the augmented mind were stacked like cards in a deck, so she started to move backwards to find the event. Nothing.

A chill began to creep up her spine. Farther and farther she searched, and still nothing. She fought to control her emotions, to control her fear. She went back and back into blank time.

Now Helen was frightened. The harder it was for her to disprove them, the more Hendricks's words seemed true. Finally, in an act of desperation, she engaged the AI companion, an aspect of the wetware that she didn't like and never used. But desperate times called for desperate measures.

Companion, she thought, *find last known encounter with peacekeeper ships.* She had never named the companion because she never thought she would need it. The desired log flashed across her visual with a time stamp. *Okay, that sounded right.*

Companion, why couldn't I locate log in my search?

- **You didn't go back far enough.** - the companion remarked.

Now her hair was almost standing straight up. She forced herself to ask the last question.

How far back?

- **744 years, 7 months, 3 days, 15 hours, and 21 minutes.** -

Oh, my God. Oh my God. This can't be real.

- **Your blood pressure is elevated and your heartbeat has become rapid,** - the companion said. - **Please concentrate on your breathing ... shall I contact emergency medical?** -

Shut up shut up you stupid thing. Disconnect wetware, override. Disconnect.

The wetware shut off and Helen sat alone in the tent for several moments. *My sister, everyone I know ... everyone I ever met. Dead. Dead for centuries.*

She simply sat there for a long time and then finally got up to find Brent. Moments later, she changed her mind and went to find Hendricks instead.

***

It had already been a strange and trying day, and Hendricks had intended to relax, alone, with a flagon of ale and a hasty meal. Now it seemed that idea was interrupted by a loud commotion outside of his tent; he recognized Helen's voice threatening his guard. Suddenly she burst into the tent with the astonished guard at her heels.

"Forgive me, Tyrr. She will not listen!" the guard stammered.

"No worries, Derric. I will speak with her," Hendricks assured the man.

"Yeah, you've got a worry all right," Helen said, her fists planted firmly on her hips. "Just who the hell do you think you are? First, you want me to accept that we can't get out of this insane world, and next, an invading army—a whole army—vanishes into thin air right in front of the whole camp." She stopped speaking for a moment and levelled her gaze at Hendricks.

"They weren't an invading army," he interjected.

"And do you tell me what the hell is going on? No, you don't. You send for Brent, and you boys have a nice chinwag while I sit alone and wonder what's going on out there." She continued to stare at him intensely. "And here I was starting to think that you are decent sort of a man, but it turns out you are just a man."

Hendricks was a bit stunned by this. He knew that what Helen was saying was true; he had called for Brent and made the mistake of assuming they would both arrive. He had been among the Zingaris so long now he was adopting their otherwise sexist overtones. Was he losing touch with his twenty-sixth century self? This would never happen to Jones; she had already outlawed Miceen's more barbarous customs.

He looked back at Helen, and he wiped the frown off his face before he spoke. "I am sorry. I should have called on both of you. There is really no excuse for it." Hendricks walked over to a corner of the tent and silently gestured to a chair. He just stood there for a moment and Helen nodded her approval. He picked up the chair and brought it closer. He put it down and gestured for her to sit down and finally she did.

He suddenly realized that in spite of being tired, he welcomed her company. They sat together and talked for a time, mostly about the appearance of the Auxconites and events of the day. Helen's mood softened as they sat and talked.

"These people have been living in the maintenance corridors and other outer sections of the world ship for, how long?" she asked.

"Well, this has been going on for over seven centuries at least; it's kind of hard to get an accurate measure of time as it has passed for the *Crimson Star*. The best that Jones and I could do was try to count the generations as they were recorded by the Miceenians. They, of all the peoples in here, have probably done the best job of keeping a recorded history.

"They began their history when they rebelled against Magnus Jupiter. It gets kind of sketchy in the period between that and the time the Olympias avatar stepped in to help guide them. Somewhere between six and seven centuries is as close as I can get.

"I wasn't really buying that time travel story at first. Then I found a way to check on it. I know exactly how much time has elapsed," Helen said. She went on to explain about her wetware, how it was otherwise useless in here, but how she had measured the time difference.

Hendricks was impressed, and his admiration for Helen jumped up another notch. They sat together without talking for a time then, and it was plainly obvious to both of them that they felt a certain physical tension in the air. The feeling, as unescapable as magnetic attraction, did its work.

Before long, they kissed. Both of them were a bit surprised at the speed with which the feelings were coming upon them, although neither of them would have denied that the attraction was there. Helen wasn't the type to fall into a relationship fast—certainly not at the speed this was moving, and yet it felt right. It felt like shelter in a storm.

Soon, Hendricks turned down the lamps and closed the inside flap of the tent for the night.

The guard who stood outside the Tyrr's tent noticed the muffled sounds of passion from inside the dark tent. Whatever the issue had been with this woman, it had obviously been resolved.

"Good to be the Tyrr," the guard muttered under his breath.

* * *

Far away across the continent-sized habitat in Necropolis, Saturn and Simon stood beside the somewhat modified biobed. Many days of trial and error with the machine itself and some interesting but strange conversations with Saturn had led Simon to the first real success with the repairs. Now they could really test it. How?

Saturn, who seemed to possess an odd understanding of many of the principles of the technology, had insisted on some very radical modifications to the machine. They made no sense to Simon, and when he asked about this, he was simply told to have some faith.

Simon was almost startled when Saturn gave him a clap on the back and said, "It only seems right that you should be the first one to use the regenerator." That was what Saturn always called it.

If he felt bold enough, Simon would explain what the machine was and what it had been its intended use. Saturn would listen patiently and then either ignore him or make a comment like, "It needed many repairs."

A sudden nervousness ran through Simon. There was something in Saturn's voice.

"Please climb up onto the bed, Simon, and let's see if the machine can regenerate your lost hand."

"But it can't do that!" Simon insisted. "I've tried to tell you—"

Saturn turned to look at him, reached out, and put a powerful hand on Simon's shoulder. He squeezed slightly and Simon let out a gasp. Fear caused him to break out in a sweat. His mind was a torn-up thing by now, and he was caught between his admiration for this more than human being and his fear of him. He had no choice but to comply with the command as he knew all too well what happened to those who defied Saturn. There was a ring of crucifixes around the city itself; many of the crosses still contained the rotting remains of the leaders of the last uprising. Simon climbed into the biobed.

Saturn poked at the command console, and the machine came alive. It scanned Simon in a flash and immediately focused on the arm with the missing hand. Heat poured into his arm, rising until it became painful but not unbearable as the machine administered pain blockers. The original design as an emergency medical biobed was still functioning beneath the weird new modifications that Saturn had been applying.

Simon watched in disbelief as a hand began to grow out of the severed part of his lower arm. It began as weak and shrivelled, and then changed to small and weak. It grew more but remained weak, and then it finally formed up into an almost perfect replacement for his original hand.

Simon felt a great elation as he looked at his new hand. The elation turned to fear and then horror as the hand continued to grow; the musculature of the hand became exaggerated and settled down into a very strong-looking, grossly oversized hand. The new limb was a beastly and powerful part of his person now.

Simon felt a scream rising in his throat. He could feel the power of the new hand. Part of himself welcomed this bizarre new appendage in spite of the fact that he had no idea how this minor miracle was achieved.

"Behold my new right-hand man, Simon the great!" Saturn said and began to laugh.

The scream in Simon's throat broke then and after rising an octave or two, turned into a peal of crazed laughter. The two stood in the room in a tower in Necropolis and after they had finished laughing, discussed how they intended to conquer the rest of Terraroma.

If there had ever been any chance of Simon regaining sanity in light of the current event, it was gone for good now. That sanity was replaced by twisted dedication to the horrible being who Simon now acknowledged as his lord and master. Together they would shake the very foundations of this spinning world, lost in time and lost in space.

Simon felt a strange new sense of freedom coming over him. Here in this strange land and at the side of this wicked being, he would finally receive the respect he had always felt that he'd been denied in life. Here, men and women would kneel before him. He thought of Brent, who had so casually cooked the stump of his arm. Brent who had brought them here. Yes, there would be a reckoning of sorts with Brent one day in the future as well.

13

THE GREAT COUNCIL OF MICEEN

TIME PASSED AND the newcomers settled into life within the Zingaris camp. Brent found these nomadic folk to be friendly and inviting. In spite of himself, he made a bid to be accepted into one of the twelve great houses that made up the general organization of Zingaris society. Membership in the houses, arranged based on the ancient European zodiac, wasn't based in any way upon a person's birthdate. This surprised Brent when he saw the way time and the calendar were laid out in Terraroma; it came close to the solar year of Earth, which had been used by the original habitants of the *Crimson Star*. His acceptance, or rejection, would be based on what skills a person brought to the house. He had made his bid for Lion House at Hendricks's advice. This house was known for its building and organizational skills. Hendricks had suggested a twenty-sixth-century man might have some new tricks to offer Lion House.

Helen, who had moved into the Tyrr's tent with Hendricks, was instantly accepted into the house of the Tyrr, which loosely translated into Taurus, with a bull symbol on their insignia. She was instantly accepted and treated with respect as Tyrr Consort although she did get the occasional dirty look from some of the women who had hoped to achieve the position of honour she now held.

At last, the time arrived for the Great Council of Terraroma. Oniman had been given the correct time and location as promised. To everyone's surprise, it was within the city walls of Miceen. The Good Goddess herself would be attending this very important meeting of peoples; this had never been done before in the history of Terraroma.

Hendricks was more than a bit apprehensive about seeing the goddess/Jones. They had not spoken in person for years. Their last face to face meeting had been angry and was a painful memory to both of them. God knows that they had both been through enough. However, current events were disturbing enough to override anyone's personal feelings; there was more at stake here than any one disagreement between parties. The work that would be done here could decide the next stage in the histories of the peoples of Terraroma. They would have to work together to oppose the threat of the alien who still haunted the world ship.

To make matters more difficult, many of the different groups saw the problems in different ways and defined the players in sometimes complicated ways. The hillmen, for example, believed they had come to seek the extradition of the war criminal, Marcellus. In the beginning, at least, the delegates would likely have come with different goals in mind.

There was a settling in period of two days for the different delegates to arrive and an arrival schedule to make sure they did not arrive at the same time. Miceen was playing host to this new venture and had limited resources to accommodate everyone at the same time. Hendricks didn't believe that for a minute; to him, Miceen was now like the superpowers of old Earth history. They liked to help, but for all their peaceful talk, they had the biggest and most powerful army in all the land.

Denzeel was miserable about coming to Miceen; he had suffered a bad break with his wife five years earlier after the fall of Olympias. Denzeel's wife, Laurenna, had felt he should retire from soldiering completely. He found the prospect unappealing, and with the added fact that the children had reached adult age and moved away, the two could not reconcile. Denzeel's wife left and went to live with her sister. In the end, Denzeel had followed Hendricks, and together the pair set out for new adventures, which ultimately ended in Hendricks becoming Tyrr of the Zingaris. However, that is another story. Denzeel was happy when the actual talks began fairly soon after arriving.

Time had passed quickly once they were inside the city walls of Miceen; however, Denzeel spent some time observing the changes that had been made to the city since the reign of the Good Goddess had begun. He was amazed at how much the ancient city had been beautified while Brent and Helen were simply aghast at the size of the place. The contrast between Miceen and the city they had been rescued from was not lost on them either.

Hendricks's group had the largest number of people who would actually be in the talks: Himself, Denzeel, Brent, and Helen. A large banquet hall on the ground level of the palace had been cleared for the event. A large semi-circular table was set up with chairs; it could accommodate the group comfortably. Security was provided, of course, by Miceen's spit polish army.

There is a lot of Jones in this Good Goddess, Hendricks thought as they took their place at the great table.

The entire meeting would consist of delegates from the Zingaris, Miceen, and the Gar-Tu, a population of hillmen from the north of Terraroma, closer to Augustine. The language that the hillmen used was an odd dialect of old English and was often confusing to people meeting them for the first time. The term *Gar-Tu*, for example, meant both leader and also referred to them collectively as a people. Finally, the Auxconites, who were the surprise of the year to the whole habitat, were the last group to arrive. They turned heads as they entered the city; all three delegates wore long white robes and had shaven heads. They resembled Miceenian priests to some extent, but it was their very pale complexions that caught people's attention.

The Good Goddess would be the last to enter, and the talks were ready to begin any moment. Helen sat beside Hendricks, which wasn't a big surprise; they didn't try to hide their relationship, but they didn't talk about it, either. Denzeel was next, and then Brent. Oniman and Onyxis, Gar-Tu and Tor, the hillmen's second in command, were up the other side, while the Good Goddess would sit in a position where she could see everyone else clearly.

People were slightly pensive, although the kind Miceenians had made every effort to make them comfortable. Quarters were provided for as long as was needed. A grand reception was held for the visitors, with a promise of more later on. Afterward, great buffets were provided, to everyone's delight, and Gar-Tu and Tor easily ate half of the spread. Finally, a man came out and announced the coming of the Good Goddess, and at last she arrived, flanked by two centurions.

Hendricks immediately noticed that she was taller than both; this was another example of the odd transformation she had undergone. The "goddess" was a good three inches taller than she had been before merging with the world ship's AI matrix.

She impassively walked out and took her place. Her golden-coloured skin and jet-black orb eyes were unsettling to everyone for a moment. Hendricks was taken aback, although he had seen her before; he recalled the shock he'd felt the first time seeing her after her bizarre resurrection. She was dressed in simple clothing, a skirt and a tunic. Some dark lines on her gold skin stretched out from under the clothes; these were scars from her final battle with Olympias that somehow couldn't be repaired. Her features were exactly those of Macy Jones, the regular soldier girl who wound up here by misadventure.

Helen and Brent were completely aghast. They had only seen Saturn, who was strange enough, but this woman, this creature, was something else again. Now the odd and regal woman had risen to her feet again and was addressing the assembled people. Aides and companions who had been gathered around the room were told to leave; only those who spoke for their people or had a significant contribution to make would be allowed to stay.

"Again, I need to thank everyone for coming to these talks. I feel that it bodes well for us all that we would make this effort and come together," said the Good Goddess. She proceeded to thank each delegate and introduced them by name, finally adding, "Many of you I have never met before and only know your names by where you sit. Others go way back, and it is good to see you." She smiled directly at Denzeel, who almost jumped in his seat.

She continued. "Each of us has a reason to be here which is connected to what is happening in the north, in Augustine. We all recognize the danger that is growing as this person called Saturn becomes more powerful each day. Beware! he is not what he appears to be; there is an elemental spirit alive in this one which is evil. It is evil and it is a liar who exists to drink the pain of the innocent as a drunkard devours his wine. I know this completely and I beseech you to beware.

"We know that in the north, the tyranny of Saturn has reached out into the surrounding lands; small hamlets and villages that had once operated peacefully and with anonymity are now firmly under the boot. The boot of General Marcellus, as far the villagers are concerned, and we have been petitioned for compensation.

"In the beginning, I had believed that perhaps it was Marcellus, for I knew him to be a fiercely ambitious warrior. Had he gone mad? Did he think that the time had come for him to rule a kingdom of his own?"

Gar-Tu gave out a growl and hammered a fist on the table. "He calls himself Saturn, but it is Marcellus! Many have seen him when he and his dogs come invading our lands!"

The Good Goddess merely looked over at the hillman after this outburst. She leaned toward him and fixed the man in the gaze of her unnaturally dark eyes. He got the unspoken message, clearly, for he sat back in his chair and folded his arms in front of him.

"Before I say any more, I would like to hear from all of you. I think that we should share our experiences of these things openly in the hope that we can learn and ponder a plan of action." She sat down then, and the room stayed quiet for a moment.

"Perhaps we could hear from the Auxconites? Oniman, I would like to know how you fit into all of this. I was genuinely surprised to learn of your people, although, in retrospect, it is not inconceivable how your culture evolved. Life finds a way. Could you address us?"

Oniman rose quietly and gave a couple of hasty half bows to the room before he began to talk. He looked pale in the company of others who lived under the sun line. He spoke in a low but clear tone.

"Thank you, Minerva, as my people call you, Good Goddess, or Captain Jones, if you please. Whatever title you hold, you are the one who slew Olympias, and we hold you in high esteem. Hendricks, too, is held in high esteem among our people for he defeated Magnus Jupiter; his actions were foretold in our beliefs and while it would take too long to divulge all of our beliefs, suffice to say both of your deeds are highly significant to our people. We bow to you.

"Our history has been bloody and varied. Much was lost to us. God has bestowed new gifts upon us to compensate for our years of suffering. We have been open with you and have pledged not to use any illusions inside of the walls of Miceen. To be clear to anyone who is here and does not know of our skills as of yet, we have the ability to cloud the minds of people, used in self-defence, as well as the ability to project images into the mind of others. Most importantly, we are pacifists. We will not do violence against others."

"So, what good are you gonna be against an army, armed with steel and fire?" Gar-Tu burst out suddenly out of place.

The Good Goddess stepped in at this point, raising her long golden arm high. "Order!" she commanded and turned to Gar-Tu directly. "My friend from the northern hills forgets that we have a way to do things, and you too will get of be heard in your turn. I politely ask you to allow Oniman to finish his statement."

"Thank you, Good one," he continued. "Gar-Tu only illustrates our problem. We are pacifists and would normally merely make sure Saturn did not learn of our existence. He does not know of us now, and it would be strategic to keep it that way. We have come forth to all assembled because we recognize the threat that is Augustine, and that is Saturn. Our last information about Saturn was that he was officially declaring himself a god and that the city of Augustine was to be renamed Necropolis."

This drew a reaction from the assembly. Oniman paused for a moment before continuing. "We realize that in time Saturn will become too strong. You say that he is the same thing that came before as the avatars Magnus Jupiter and Olympias and that this is an alien thing. It can be no good for God's Seed or its mission.

"In short, we wish to help in this crisis and are open to suggestion on the role we can play."

"Thank you, Oniman," the Good Goddess said. "Now could I call upon Gar-Tu and the voices of the northern hillmen." Every head at the table turned to look at Gar-Tu, dressed as he was in animal skins, with his long hair and scruffy beard. He was outlandish even beside the Zingaris, who dressed for their environment in convertible desert wear. He had not been permitted to bring his stone axe into the talking chamber. This had been a great bone of contention, settled only when he bestowed the axe to another Gar-tu.

Gar-Tu stood and spoke. "People of the Council, thank you for inviting us and the hillmen salute you!" He thumped each huge fist against his chest in turn and continued. "My purpose for coming here today is clear, and I fear different from what you perhaps think. We want the criminal Marcellus, a man who was in the employ of Olympias when he first made war on us but has now usurped Augustine."

Hendricks was on his feet now, much to his is own surprise. "I was there and that is not what happened. You are misinformed, friend. Or a liar." He was trying to contain his anger. It wasn't so easy to forget how the army he'd been riding with had been attacked by a savage group of hillmen some of whom had been riding atop coyotozen, automated animal machines. Many died that day and in Hendricks's memory, the attack from the hillmen in the campaign against Magnus Jupiter was the first blood of the war. They had fought for Magnus Jupiter, and while they had likely submitted to the tyrant out of fear, it didn't change the way he felt.

Gar-Tu turned to glare at Hendricks, his face curling into a snarl. "You calling me a liar, little desert rat?"

"The truth is a tough concept for a hillman. Maybe you remember things the way you want to?" Hendricks rose to his feet. Tension in the room was coming close to the breaking point, and Hendricks was already regretting his own words. Perhaps it had been a mistake to gather these groups together in this way; old wounds are easily opened.

"There will be order in this meeting!" The Good Goddess's voice rose to unnatural levels startling everyone gathered. She glared at Hendricks. "You who were among the first to suggest this meeting should know better. I'm disappointed, John." She turned to look at the others. "So we come to it. There is much confusion around some events over the last five years. For example," she looked a Gar-Tu, "we believe that Marcellus is dead and has been since the end of the revolution. Magnus Jupiter and Olympias were controlled by a single alien entity who we often call Loki from an Earth mythological figure, the god of mischief, a deceiver.

"At any rate, when I drove this alien out, tossing him down from heaven, you might say, he did not perish. He somehow became Marcellus. We are not sure about how this was accomplished because the alien had always used some twisted version of human tech to create a corporal body for itself. This man, who I understand raised great misery against your people, may have looked more like General Marcellus of old, but I believe that it was Loki who marched on your people."

"In truth," said Gar-Tu, "we feared reprisals for our part in the war. We believed that Magnus Jupiter would win and hoped to stay safe if we backed him early." He lowered his head at these words. "In truth, we did not believe that a man could do the things that Marcellus had done. They came and burnt down our villages and set my people to flight. They hunted us like animals, man, woman, and child. Death is preferable to being captured by these monsters, to die in the arena or be worked to death as slaves."

Murmurs filled the room at this statement.

He turned to look at Hendricks again and continued. "In truth, the change came quickly. No sooner had Magnus Jupiter been defeated when Marcellus began his campaigns against us. This was not a war but an extermination." Gar-Tu fell silent then, a haunted look in his eyes, and he bowed his head. Finally, he looked up and addressed Jones.

"We would learn more of this 'alien.' We do not know how you mean the word, but to us, it merely means 'an outsider,'" he said.

"Perhaps it would be best to think of him as a demon. Do you have a devil in your culture?" the Good Goddess asked Gar-Tu.

"There is a legend among us about an evil wind which draws back the foot that is slow. This is no natural wind, for it has purpose and malice and takes soldier or maid alike. It has no mercy," Gar-Tu replied.

"This is what we speak of; something evil that has replaced Marcellus. Now there is only Saturn! That same being who has caused so much misery all across Terraroma," the Good Goddess said. "And now we shall hear from the Zingaris and my old comrades Hendricks and Denzeel, who have managed to rescue two other travellers who have become lost in space and ultimately become stranded here."

Hendricks rose again as he was given the floor. He hesitated before speaking. Seeing Jones had unsettled him again. He would never get used to the being she had become; she was at once the woman he knew and something strange. She was both familiar and unfamiliar in the same glance.

"Thank you," he said finally, nodding to the Good Goddess. "I knew General Marcellus as well as anyone, and we fought together in two campaigns. This is not Marcellus." The statement caused a mutter to go through the assembled people once again; Hendricks was surprised to find how much authority his words carried. He spoke then of how he and Jones had come to be among them, and continued his narrative until he came to the present situation. This took a bit of time, and he omitted nothing of his adventures, including how he came to be the ruler of the Zingaris. Everyone at the meeting listened patiently as he told his tale; many knew parts, but only Denzeel knew the whole story. Even Jones, the Good Goddess, seemed surprised as she listened to how Hendricks had lived among the Zingaris as a warrior for a time until finally he challenged the leader of the desert nomads and defeated him in single combat to become the Tyrr of the Zingaris representing twelve houses and a population of approximately 15,000 people.

Hendricks called upon the others with him to speak to their roles in recent events; Brent recalled his experience with Saturn before being thrown into the arena, and Helen spoke of their eventual rescue. Oniman listened intensely, and everyone learned something new about the situation in the north of Terraroma. When Hendricks was finished speaking and directing input from the others, he sat down. The room fell silent as each person was lost in thought.

The Good Goddess asked for a two-hour recess, and all agreed, although Hendricks was sure that he heard Denzeel groan at this; he wished to leave Miceen as soon as possible. Helen told Hendricks that he had spoken well and took his hand as they exited the council chamber. Brent rolled his eyes but then smiled at the pair; a fleeting pang of jealousy passed quickly. He laughed to himself, surprised by the union but happy for Helen. Food and entertainment were provided, and the large public baths were offered. The break went quickly. All had time to relax a bit before the ringing of a bell called them back to the council.

When everyone was settled in, the Good Goddess/Jones addressed the group, "Surely we can devise a plan of action and at least coordinate our actions." "Before I accepted the responsibilities of defending Miceen, I was a soldier. I believe that the only wrong course of action here would be to do nothing. Now we must put the transgressions of our neighbours aside. The Zingaris have raided our outposts in the past, but now, with a new Tyrr, there is peace between us. Let this set an example for us all; tomorrow is the time we must focus on.

"Think, if you will, for a moment, not as part of your city or territory but as one group—we all share a common heritage, and I believe a common future. Loki, as I call it, or Saturn as it prefers, stands in the way of that future. I call it Loki because that was the name of a god in ancient times on Earth; he was a god of mischief and lies. We know that it craves to dominate all the peoples of Terraroma; we have heard enough testimony to know that it rules by fear and intimidation. To survive an invasion would likely ensure becoming a slave. And we also know this thing uses slaves to forward his own power! Again, good people, I ask you: what do we do?"

Many people started in their chairs, and it was immediately obvious there were different opinions.

Hendricks spoke without invitation in a loud and angry voice, "We should attack. Together we should march on Augustine and destroy Saturn!"

"No, we should not start a war," Oniman injected. "We would suggest espionage instead. We should find a way to destroy the thing singularly. We are pacifists, as I have said, and have no quarrel with the general population of Augustine. We will not take up arms, but we will do what we can."

"There is no time for that!" Brent burst out. "That ... that thing, that maniac up there is just itching to go to war. All he's waiting for is to gather strength, and from what I saw, he has a pretty big army. Hell, the whole goddamn place is like a barracks."

"We will fight!" Gar-Tu said and scoffed as he looked at Oniman.

The Good Goddess spoke with authority in her voice then, as a diplomat who knows that she has the strongest voice in the room. "Good friends, I feel that both ideas hold great merit. We should try to avoid wholesale slaughter and perhaps, together, we can forge a plan that uses both strategies. Let us plan together!"

And so, the group looked around at one another and after a moment, they began the task of forming a plan of action. Minutes turned to hours, but a plan was finally developed. It was decided that the whole plan should remain secret except for those within the council. Both ideas were assembled on a timeline; their collective armies would be coordinated for war, but a recon mission was planned to begin immediately. The assembled armies would gather in the northern plains above the Eastern Pass.

The goddess was happy with the results, and she dubbed the group "the First Council of Terraroma." After the council had disbanded, Hendricks and Helen remained in Miceen for another day, enjoying the hospitality.

Denzeel, however, left the city that first night. He and Oniman were to go north to where the enemy was; they left quickly and quietly to keep their purpose secret. Their mission was to go into Augustine—now called Necropolis—itself and to gather information about Saturn's strength and his plans. In addition to that, they were to find out if there was an underground rebellion that opposed Saturn; such groups had traditionally existed within the city states during the reigns of Olympias and Magnus Jupiter. It was the council's opinion that many of the citizens had become corrupted and were now wicked, but there could still be good people trapped in a bad situation. If a resistance was there, Denzeel and Oniman were charged to make contact with them.

Denzeel had not been happy with the assignment but was dedicated to Hendricks and would follow his order, whatever it might be. There was something about Oniman that didn't sit well with him although he couldn't really put his finger on what it was; the man had a strangeness about him that went beyond the cultural differences.

After the brief stay, they all departed to their consecutive groups. There was a lot of work to do.

14

NECROPOLIS RISING

BY THE TIME the Great Council of Terraroma had concluded and dispatched its spies north to Necropolis, Saturn and his subjects were pretty much prepared to start the war. They had the jump on the free people, without a doubt, and they knew that a resistance was being mounted against them, for they too had watchful eyes planted in the south. Saturn was unaware of the two men who had been sent to Necropolis; however, he wouldn't have been surprised had he known. After all, wasn't such subterfuge practically tradition in the age-old conflict between the two city states?

In Necropolis, formerly known as Augustine, the city was buzzing with activity. In the initial days following the defeat of Magnus Jupiter, early plans were drawn up to restore the city to its former glory. However, as the situation changed and General Marcellus, who was then considered the Military Governor of Augustine, began to show signs of becoming radically different, such efforts were altered. Plans for reconstruction became plans for conquest, and Marcellus declared himself the solitary ruler, dictator for life. Augustine was renamed Necropolis and not a soul dared to speak against these changes. Marcellus himself was renamed Saturanius Maximus and was declared to be a living god. With each month that passed, the once military governor, the man named Marcellus, became less and less of the man that even his own soldiers knew; the invading influence became complete until there was only Saturn, the god of Necropolis. The god of war and death.

The people who had lived their lives under the rule of Magnus Jupiter were used to a heavy-handed ruler, and had been raised from generation to generation with the twisted demon king they had always known. This was something different again; this was a conquering general from Miceen, who in fact represented Olympias, the sorceress ruler of the southern city state. The strangest twist, however, was that after Magnus Jupiter was dead, General Marcellus broke his alliance with Olympias and declared himself ruler of Augustine. The final twist was when news came that Olympias had also fallen and been replaced by a new ruler, the "Good Goddess" of Miceen. This was when Marcellus truly began to transform into the being who called himself Saturn.

To look at him directly was an unnerving experience in itself; during public experiences, Simon took efforts to improve Saturn's appearance by applying a bit of makeup to the new leader to make him appear less, well, dead. Parts of the man who was once Marcellus had begun to rot away. Worst of all was his left cheek, where bone could be seen through the failing flesh. Looking at him was like looking at death itself.

Everyone had work to do, and everyone would make a contribution to the war effort. To not participate in the preparation was a good way to wind up on a cross. Saturn would not tolerate any dissension. His laws and directions were to be followed to the letter; anyone who failed to do so was arrested and taken before the tribunal. The tribunal had a 100 percent conviction rate, and this was one of the ways that he ruled: through fear and intimidation. Finally, after months of preparation, the armies of Saturn were ready to set out on conquest.

The citizens of Necropolis knew better than to defy the new ruler; what they didn't know was the thing that ruled them was in fact the same entity that had always ruled them, the alien creature whom the spirit Vokova called Loki. The creature had survived after being pushed out of the great AI system where it had been for centuries. The hope of Jones, who had ousted the thing, was that it would return to space, to the strange other-dimensional space from where it came. But that was not what happened. It remained, disembodied within the living environment of the *Crimson Star*. It had sensed the pain and fear within General

Marcellus, who was dying of some form of consumption, or cancer, as visitors from the Sol System called such conditions.

A brief military parade was ordered, and the people of Necropolis had gathered in the arena to see Saturn's war ceremonies. Saturn himself sat in his royal balcony low enough for seasoned warriors to salute him as they passed and high enough to give everyone a glimpse of the warrior king. The battle-hardened legions of the army led the procession.

Beside Saturn in the observation box was Simon, the Hand of the King, a man now transformed. The twisted humour of the appointment did not escape the citizens, but no one would dare to laugh at the sight of the stranger with the oversize hand.

Behind the main legions came the newest recruits, who marched in formation. Only the centurions of this group saluted. They made their circuit and then the newest members fell at ease into the formation dictated to them by those centurions.

Saturn rose from his seat and the crowds cheered. He was dressed in a lavish purple robe and wore a gold circle with golden leaves adorning it. He raised a hand and the arena fell silent. Then, in a voice that may as well have been amplified but wasn't, he spoke to the people. The construction of the arena had been many years in the past and the builders of the time had designed incredible acoustics for the structure; even the most distant spectators could clearly hear the speaker.

"Citizens! People of Necropolis, the legions of Necropolis!" he cried. Cheers burst out and then fell silent again. "Beyond the walls, seven more legions await in the surrounding plains. These are the legions of Saturn, and they have risen again to defend our city! Rejoice, good citizens. We are powerful beyond measure, and now I will show you the genius of the King's Hand; the first Saturnian Air Force!" Saturn pointed high into the sky, above the arena.

Almost specks in the sky were three shapes flying around and circling above the gathering. People gasped as they saw more specks join the first three until there were fifteen in total. Slowly, the circle of specks tightened, and they began to drop lower with every circle. Finally, the gathered crowds watched in astonishment as they realized that people were flying above them in strange contraptions that made them look like great birds, who swooped around and came lower until finally they to came land in the open area of the centre of the arena. The people cheered and applauded after a fashion, but many did not. They were utterly perplexed by the sight of the fifteen flying soldiers.

Simon stood and soaked up the attention. Months earlier, even before his transformation into the Hand, he had conceived the idea of the Necropoline Air Force. Simon, with an education in engineering, had been fascinated by the physics of life in a McKendree cylinder. It was easily the greatest engineering feat of technological man beyond space travel. He had read extensively about the *Crimson Star* when he was a student, never for a moment thinking that he would end up living inside the lost world ship. He had read how one of the passions of the youth who had been part of that first generation aboard the *Crimson Star* when she set out had been hang gliding. High in the mountains of the environment the gravity was much lower and it was perfect for flying. As the flyers grew closer to the centre of the McKendree cylinder, the gravity became almost non-existent. The young daredevils could even release the gliders (although tethered to them) and perform somersaults in the air before flying back to their gliders.

Simon had explained this to Saturn and had been given permission to go into the mountains to begin the trials. The end result was the fifteen flyers who had just landed in the arena. This would give his side an advantage in the coming conflict. He saluted the crowd with his huge hand and sat back down.

"Beyond our territory, there are many who would make war on us. The witch in the south has gathered leaders from different lands together as they attempt to rally against our might." Saturn continued, turning to face another area of the arena. "This is a big world with many different people within it. We could live and let live, but why should we do this while they plan war against us? The filthy barbarians in the western hills no longer call us allies and the desert rats will have nothing to do with us.

"Do we wait, we the stronger? There is only one thing that all the people of this world understand, and that is power. Raw, merciless, naked power! And that is what every soldier knows!" The assembled forces cheered and banged on their shields. "And they know that it's their sacred duty to expand the power of our empire and to invade!" More cheers.

"Invade!" he cried again, and now the entire arena cheered. All rose to their feet and showed their devotion regardless of how they really felt. The citizens of Necropolis knew who the boss was, and they also knew what happened to dissenting voices. They also knew that if the boss made a joke, it was *funny* regardless of whether it actually was or not. If your neighbour got crucified, he *deserved* it, regardless of whether he was guilty of anything or not. Most of the people assembled had known little else than war; peace was only an extended break before the next campaign, the endless struggle for control of all Terraroma.

Saturn's speech went on for a while longer, and the gathered population cheered him on. After the speech was finally over, the daily entertainment commenced with executions and gladiatorial games. He knew full well that some of the assembled citizens were repulsed by these bloody spectacles, and he basked in the emotions of fear and terror, such fleeting delicacies that they were. War was coming, and that was what he truly loved, that orgy of blood and hate.

The sun line dimmed as it stretched away from the northlands, and Saturn grinned his awful grin in the gathering darkness.

15

TYRR OF THE ZINGARIS

HENDRICKS AND HELEN had returned to the Zingaris camp a few hours earlier, and Hendricks had been cursing himself for being a damn fool for at least a couple of those hours. He was thinking that he'd been spending so much time concerning himself with other matters that he'd neglected his responsibilities with the Zingaris. He was, after all, Tyrr.

In their absence, a warrior named Drago had called for a vote. He would personally challenge Hendricks for the leadership position of Tyrr. Drago represented a group of people who were losing confidence in Hendricks in light of the incident with the Auxconites. One of Hendricks' supporters came to him and claimed that the people Drago claimed to represent had been manipulated by him. It was not a fair challenge, the man said. Also, Drago's supporters were reasonable men and would likely back off if they were made to understand the situation better. However, it didn't matter now; the vote had gone to the elder council, a group of older, respected warriors called the Desert Wolves, and they had upheld the challenge. The die was cast; Hendricks would have to face Drago in one-on-one combat. To the death.

Helen was horrified by this sudden, barbaric turn of events and for the first time, Hendricks was worried if their relationship had the legs for the kind of world they were living in. She knew he had ascended to this leadership in the same way. Unfortunately, there was little time to worry about that now, as the challenge was required to be met as soon as possible. As soon as the sun line had set in the far south behind the mountains, the battle was set to be fought in firelight, in the twilight of the day. In Zingaris culture, the loser represented the falling sun, and the victory represented the returning sun, fierce and hot in the new day. He would rise the next day, take command of the Zingaris, and life would continue.

The Zingaris would sing of legendary leadership battles that lasted till dawn came again. In his experience, most single combat situations were over quick. Some could go on a bit, but it was usually fast. Hendricks sat quietly in his tent to prepare himself. Helen had left, and he had already decided to deal with that later. If he survived. He made himself as still as he could, taking control of his breathing, and with the skill of a lion tamer, he forced his heart rate down, down until the calmness began to sharpen his vision. Time slowed. He was ready.

Hendricks walked out of his tent and down to the designated place. Burning torches formed a large circle. The entire encampment had gathered for this; it was one of the most important events in Zingaris life. He entered the circle at one end as allies scrambled to show their support for him by gathering near him. He smiled and nodded to his people, those who had been faithful from the beginning, and they cheered and chanted his name.

Directly across the circle was Drago. Beside him were his supporters and a man whom Hendricks recognized as Felix Gru. He was a recent arrival, and Hendricks wondered if the man was on a mission. An assassination mission for Saturn, perhaps.

Am I becoming paranoid? Hendricks asked himself and then let out a small laugh. *How could I not be paranoid when I'm about to face someone who wants to kill me and take my job?* He would look into Felix later; right now, he had Drago to worry about.

A representative of the elders' council, Misculus, walked into the centre of the circle and said a few words. Misculus was old, grey, and bent, but as he handed the two men the ceremonial weapons—small double-sided knives, three and a half inches with a black hilt—he walked straight as an arrow and puffed up with pride. Misculus took this very seriously. Each man was now equally armed, and the fight could begin. Misculus stepped out of the circle, and the fight began.

The two men began to circle each other, both right-handed and holding their blade in that hand. Hendricks had the advantage in height and weight, but Drago was perhaps the faster of the two. That was not to say that Hendricks wasn't fast. He was still extremely quick.

Drago went on the attack quickly and went for a slash to the face.

Hendricks twisted out of the way and countered with a judo kick to the ribs.

Drago took the force of the kick with a roll to the left.

Hendricks tried to take advantage of the moment and came in with a plunging cut.

Drago was too fast and caught his wrist, struggling to his feet. The two men grappled for a time, neither able to gain an advantage. Drago tried another tactic and fell backwards, pulling Hendricks with him. As Hendricks fell forward, Drago kicked upward, catching him in the stomach and flipping him up and over onto his back. Drago moved as fast as lightning to come over and stab down into Hendricks. That is not how it worked out, however.

Drago had underestimated Hendricks's greater height and longer reach. Hendricks extended his arm as fast as a viper and plunged his dagger into Drago's throat. Drago continued to fall forward with the strength of the stab, and Hendricks twisted almost a second too late and received a nasty slash in his shoulder. He let out a howl, a painful-sounding cry of triumph.

Drago was dead before he hit the ground. Hendricks shoved the body off him and climbed to his feet. He pulled the ceremonial dagger out of Drago and held the bloody blade up into the air.

"We should perhaps find better ways to solve our differences! Now I have one less soldier, a good capable man, to help us meet the threat to the north!" Hendricks was dizzy with adrenalin as he shouted out his thoughts. He knew it wouldn't go over well with some, especially the elders' council. *Why do I care what they think?* he asked himself. *If we don't deal with Loki or Saturn or whoever, then we are gonna have bigger problems.*

He took a deep breath and continued while he had everyone's attention. He was calmer now. "Desert wolves! I claim my right as Tyrr to continue as Tyrr. I claim my right in blood!" He shook the blade in the air, droplets of blood falling on some spectators in the front.

"When the sun rises tomorrow, I claim a renewed leadership. We break camp at dawn, and we head north. We shall cross the Great Desert, and songs will be sung of our deeds!" A mutter went through the crowd, then turned to applause and then to cheers. And then the cheers were like thunder, and Hendricks had never heard this from the Zingaris before. He felt good, better than he had for a while. His confidence was restored.

"The warriors should drink to Drago's bravery tonight," Hendricks said as his wound was cleaned and dressed. *That was a pretty good PR line*, he thought. Drago was brave but stupid; it was rare for someone to challenge a Tyrr that early on in their leadership. Even if Drago had been successful, someone else would probably have come after him before long. Traditionally, a Tyrr wasn't challenged until they were older. If Hendricks had fallen, it might have created a rift among the Zingaris and that would have been very badly timed.

When Hendricks returned to his tent, Helen had already returned, and this surprised him in a good way. He smiled at the sight of her, but she stood shock still, her arms folded around her.

"I knew somehow that you would be okay," she said to him. "I wanted to be angry with you to protect me from the fear of losing you. But then I realized that I knew you would win, I don't know why I was so sure of it, but I was. I came back here; I couldn't watch the fight."

Hendricks just stood there for a moment. He hadn't expected her to say something like that.

"Life is hard here, Helen," he said at last. "You have to be strong to survive here, and I know that you can do that because I know what you did in the arena. Death is always with us here, but the old Desert Wolves say that is good counsel. We do what we have to, to live. We don't have to like it."

"I just don't want to have to do that. But you're right, I can." Helen let her arms fall at her sides. She looked sad and bowed her head. He wanted to go to her immediately but wasn't sure how he'd be received.

Helen looked up at him then and said, "I don't want to talk about this anymore, at least not tonight." She smiled.

Hendricks came forward and put his arms around her. The attraction between them that had remained unspoken until that moment now found expression. A deep, overwhelming wave of desire washed over them both, and they forgot about all else. Eventually, when the lamps had burnt low, Helen slept.

Hendricks lay awake for a long time, thinking. He had dodged another bullet as the old expression went. *How long,* he wondered, *could his good fortune hold out in this mad, savage world?* He was through trying to deny his feelings for Helen. Holding the position that he did within Zingaris society, he could have had any of the women he wanted, and their families would have been honoured. For Hendricks, however, such matters were governed by the heart and not by the local politics.

Hendricks admitted to himself what his heart already knew: he loved Helen with all of his heart.

* * *

The process of breaking camp began at dawn. Hendricks met with the captains, or house fathers, as they were called. It amazed Hendricks that the zodiac signs were being used. Even by the time of the *Crimson Star*'s launch, the ancient and archaic old European zodiac system was half forgotten and certainly not taken too seriously. A strange footnote in history even then, it had survived down through the centuries at least to help organize these desert nomads. All knowledge of the birthday reference had disappeared. It was simply Capricorn House or Scorpio House. Symbolically, anyway, some of the old attributes of the signs remained in the banners or symbols. Leo House, for example, had a stylized lion on their banner, yet there were no lions in Terraroma. Lions were a legend, a mythological creature, as far as the people were concerned. Tigers, by contrast, did roam close to the large southern forests.

"We shall travel west to the place where the Great Desert is thinnest, and we will cross over onto the plains where the Gar-Tu live," Hendricks said to them, which raised a few eyebrows. There was a location in the west where he could tap the power of the ship itself and hence recharge the laser rifle and pistol. As a matter of fact, Hendricks had the weapons, both of them, and that was his true purpose for crossing the Great Desert at the location they were.

The Good Goddess was in touch with the entire ship, at least in one way or another. That is not to say that she was omniscient. Not at all, but she could look in anywhere at any time if she decided to concentrate on somewhere or someone. She had discovered areas of the outer ship that were still habitable. She knew a location where the modern weapons that she and Hendricks had brought aboard could be recharged. She had told Hendricks about the charge port, functional but possibly buried in sand.

The old wolves had grumbled as they did about everything, but this time it was an old superstition about ghosts that haunted the badlands, an area close to where they would be travelling. "We'll deal with them if we encounter them," Hendricks had told the old wolves. It was a hard life, the Zingaris way, and he was beginning to wonder if he didn't deserve something better; then again, becoming Tyrr had been exactly what he'd needed some years ago when he was trying to reconcile the fact that he couldn't get back home, back to the Sol System, Earth, reality.

Hendricks ran through the general plan with his captains and, of course, the old wolves. "The Zingaris will cross the desert in the west, close to the badlands where it is thinnest, and then turn east until they meet with Gar-Tu. We have an ally among the ranks of the Gar-Tu; there will be no treachery from the hillmen. Brent is a comrade of old, and he already represents us in Gar-Tu's ranks. We are to be allies and work together to bring down Necropolis because it has become a vile and wretched place. If there are any good souls left in that place, then they are enslaved." He paused and looked around at the faces he knew—Rikkos, Gais, and old Vane. They were the main players, and he saw no sign of disagreement. He continued.

"The Good Goddess and the army of Miceen will be marching north right now. We'll coordinate with the others, and three armies will smash Necropolis. There is no time to waste. Let us ride!" The group broke up then, and the captains ran off to get their people moving.

Soon, the Zingaris were on the move. They had been travelling for about two weeks before they arrived where the Great Desert was said to begin. The Great Desert might not be considered a desert in, say, Martian terms. It wasn't the Gobi on Earth, either. What it was, in fact, an enormous wasteland that stretched all the way around the circumference of the habitat. From one side of the mountain range, all the way around to the other side. There was no life there. It was like a desert that way. Even if the soil had had any nutrients, they had been blasted out of it long ago. It was like the surface of a moon: barren, arid. Sometimes, in twilight, it could be very spooky. When the sun line was distant, what light there was just hung on, bouncing around on the empty basin until the last possible moment, and then the dark came on fast like great bat's wings covering the light.

The first night in the desert was a bit unnerving for Helen and for even more than a few of the Zingaris who had been on the desert but never stayed long enough to spend the night. It was an eerie place once the sun line was far enough for deep twilight to set in; the ground itself seemed to turn a strange dark blue colour. During one dark sun line set, Hendricks and Helen stood just outside the camp and looked west toward the mountain range. The Blue Mountains, they were called, and for good reason. The distant range was a metallic blue colour at this time, and it looked like something out of a Salvador Dali painting. Surreal.

"Why don't the mountains screw up the spin of the habitat? How can it tolerate the weight all on one part of the habitat?" Helen asked Hendricks.

A big grin broke on his face when she asked this. "I used to wonder the same thing when I first got on this mad carnival ride. Jones unravelled that mystery when she first searched for what the Miceenians called the Caves of Knowledge. The mountains are hollow. As a matter of fact, there's a transportation system inside them. The Auxconites must know about this. Maybe they even use it. They have a very odd view of technology. The other races in Terraroma see any tech as magic, but the Auxconites know better. They are one strange people."

"Those people are creepy if you ask me," Helen said. "Bald, pale as death, and those robes they wear. Creepy. I don't know if I trust them completely."

"Well, Denzeel is out there with Oniman right now. They could be in Necropolis by now. He can take care of himself, I'm sure," Hendricks said.

With a gesture from Helen the pair turned and began to walk back into the Zingaris camp. Their shadows, looking a very deep purple hue, swung around them with the motion and then stretched out behind them.

Haunted, Helen thought. *This damn place looks haunted.* Soon they reached the camp with its bright lamps and various coloured tents. Helen shook off the eerie feeling of the wasteland.

After a few more miles they were deep in the Great Desert. There was no sound but the wind and the creatures within the caravan. The main animals that travelled with them were camels and horses. Other livestock moved with them, for the caravan was like a town in motion. Pigs, chickens, and goats. The surface of the land had been hard packed at first, but now they were in actual sand. Small dunes slowed their passage, and later, although the land levelled out, dust devils whirled around and harassed them. A sandstorm was coming.

When the storm finally arrived, Hendricks ordered a full stop. They dug in to wait it out. The wind gave a low moan as the storm kept going for two solid days and threatened to go into a third. The winds diminished but didn't stop, visibility improved, but some blowing sand still plagued them. Finally, after consulting the map that the Good Goddess had given him, Hendricks signalled the advance.

The caravan began to move again. Now they travelled in a northeastern direction. This was really a path untravelled, as there was never a reason for anyone to go the way they were travelling. Hendricks figured they were maybe a day away from where he was looking for the access port. Jones, the goddess, claimed that way back before the *Crimson Star* met with disaster, there was a power station there where people brought everything from personal vehicles to farm equipment to get charged up. He could easily recharge the weapons and a couple of charge packs as well.

Hendricks was riding up front of the caravan when disaster struck. He'd had his head bowed in the wind when suddenly the ground began to shake violently. Horses reared up, and camels bolted in any direction. This lasted for several seconds, and just as Hendricks had brought his horse under control, he thought, *I've never heard of earthquakes here.*

Why would there be any? The shaking suddenly stopped, and he heard people crying and shouting down the line of the caravan.

Hendricks turned his horse around and rode toward the commotion at a respectable speed. People were rushing toward the event; cries for help were coming from the south side of the caravan. Others jumped out of Hendricks's way as he rode like the wind down the line. Finally, he was close enough for his keen eyes to behold the event.

Without warning, a sinkhole of considerable size opened up right under people's feet; they'd later discovered that forty-three people were sucked into the sinkhole so quickly that nothing could be done for them. They were gone. All Hendricks knew as he arrived at the hole was that two people, a youth and a child, were hanging on for dear life some fifteen feet down the gaping new hole in the ground. The boy was hanging onto some kind of rock formation, his legs kicking above the gapping nothing below. The child was hanging onto the youth, the little arms around his neck; she was terrified.

Hendricks didn't know what the hell was going on, but he knew he had to act. He dismounted and ran over to a group of men who were trying to fashion ropes to pull the two up. He looked down at the situation for a moment and then started giving orders. Everyone worked fast and hard. Ropes were fashioned to stakes that were driven deep into the ground. Hendricks tied one rope around his waist and gathered up two more in his arms.

He was going to do this kamikaze style; the just slightly lighter gravity made such acts a bit easier to pull off. Looking like he had gone batshit crazy, he began to run as fast as he could. When he reached the edge, he jumped as far out over the hole as he could. If the rope broke, he was done, and he knew it; there would be no recovery then.

The rope held, and Hendricks began to breathe again. He swung down toward the wall of the hole, bouncing back out a couple of times before settling down. His leg pushed him out while the rope held his weight. The kids were just above him, off to his left. He looked around and began to move closer to the pair. They were pretty happy to see him. The child, a girl, almost lost her grip around the youth's neck and Hendricks's heart skipped a beat as the child scrambled to get a better grip. She was okay.

Slowly, he moved along the loose wall until he was right below them. He signalled to the men above, who held the rope by both calling up and yanking on the line. They got the message, and he began to rise upward. Finally, he reached the kids.

The little girl began to cry as he fastened a rope around her so she could be lifted to safety. She rose up, tears and all, as Hendricks worked on the other rope for the youth. The boy gave him a big grin when it was his turn, and he was lifted up to safety. The kid was having a wild day: watching people falling into the sinkhole and almost going down himself, then hanging onto dear life with a child on his back, to finally being rescued, not just by anybody, but by the Tyrr himself! The youngster would have some bragging rights for some time to come.

When it was all over and a camp had been struck, they would stay in the area for one night, hold a quick ceremony in the morning, and then break camp. Even the people lost would understand this because they were Zingaris themselves:

"*Linger not in the grasslands or the desert,*
Lest the wind draws back the foot that is slow."

The old Desert Wolves would mutter solemnly as they finally broke camp to move on. They had all met the night before: the old wolves, the house fathers, and of course, the Tyrr. They discussed the events that had fallen upon them, and they made plans to help the families who had lost loved ones. Some thought that this was a malicious attack from an evil demon, perhaps the very demon they marched against. Others said that it was an omen of trouble ahead. Hendricks insisted that this was really what it appeared to be, a tragic accident.

After some discussion regarding these and other pressing issues, Hendricks decided to use the opportunity to announce the next steps in their journey. He knew that it wouldn't go over well. *Time for some of those leadership qualities Jones said I've discovered*, he thought as he prepared to speak.

"Brave ones, I have words to say directly to the ears of the brave," Hendricks formally said to the assembled people. "We are close to the place I have spoken of, so we will make camp for perhaps three nights at our next stop.

"I must go alone into the desert, and I ask the old wolves to indulge me this time and to be patient. This mission will make us strong and prepared to fight the evil ahead. I invoke my power as Tyrr to override any traditions which present a barrier. I cannot express enough how important this mission is. I am telling you this now, and I will not make any announcement when I depart. I do not wish to alarm the general body of the Zingaris. It is enough that we ride to war."

There would be objections, and he waited for them, but to his surprise, there was only one. Perhaps his rescue of the kids had bought him more credibility than he realized.

"Tyrr! This is beyond reason!" cried Maskis, the house father of Scorpius House. "Our leader is to run off and leave his people in the middle of the desert? In all of our scrolls and in all our memories, no Tyrr has ever done this. It will not be seen well by the people."

Maskis was a good man, and Hendricks liked him. He cared very much for the well-being of the people and less for his own personal glory; this is perhaps why only he spoke up at that moment.

Hendricks walked over and put a hand on Maskis' shoulder. "Then perhaps it is best that they don't know," he said quietly. "You are an honest man, Maskis, and I ask you to take me on my word; I would not do this if there was any other way. It is best that fewer people know."

He turned and addressed the whole assembly then. "I'm counting on all of you to keep the people safe and happy in my absence, and I am naming Maskis as my right hand in my absence. He will have the last word. Does everyone understand this?"

Hendricks looked around, and everyone voiced their understanding. Maskis stood there with his mouth hanging open.

"Tyrr," he began.

"No objections, Maskis. You are the man," Hendricks said firmly.

Maskis nodded and bowed his head in agreement. "As for the rest of you," he continued. "None shall question his authority in my absence. Is that clear?"

And that was that.

***

The next day, after the camp was made, the Zingaris were settled for an extended stay. This was greeted fairly well by the general population, who were not unhappy at staying down for a couple of days. It meant a chance for some recreation that couldn't happen when the whole camp had to pull up stakes in the morning.

Hendricks slipped out of camp near sunset the first day. As he had been preparing to leave, Helen had laughed aloud at his appearance. He looked like a cross between a cowboy and a desert nomad (which, of course, he was). The hat, a keepsake from his old life, had originally had a wide brim that ran around the bottom, but rain and sun had caused the brim to curl up like an old-fashioned cowboy hat. White cloth hung out the bottom of the hat, and his eyes were covered by his own special desert goggles, an invention of his own creation. The glasses were only needed in a sandstorm, and the style was copied by many Zingaris.

He set out finally on a good horse with saddlebags full of water gourds and other provisions. The eerie feeling of the twilight was not lost on him, but he feared his imagination less than a usurper with a sharp knife; he ignored the oddly shifting purple shadows that danced below him. Soon the camp was lost from sight, and he was glad to make quick progress. His empty laser pistol was in one bag and several drained power packs in another. There was no point in hauling the other advanced weapon, the laser rifle along on the trip. It stayed back at camp, safely stored in a place only he knew.

He was far away from the camp by full darkness, and he didn't stop that first night; whenever alone in the desert, he preferred to find shelter and rest during the day. As he rode, he tried to imagine what this world ship had been like before the disaster that wiped out all modern methods and comforts. Well, this wasteland certainly wasn't here back then. This place, the western-most arm of the Great Desert, always looked to Hendricks like a great scar across the face of the habitat. Now, as he travelled into it in darkness, he began to notice aspects of the landscape that he hadn't really paid attention to during the daylight.

His horse, Shep, had been with him for months now, since before the Great Council. The two of them proceeded at a slow trot. The landscape began to change again about halfway through the night. Hard, jagged rocks littered the way, and Hendricks had to dismount and lead Shep slowly through the rubble. Tall, strangely shaped rock formations rose up around him as they moved slowly forward. Hendricks found that he couldn't help but think about that first disaster and how devastating it must have been.

Years ago, at the time of the fall of Magnus Jupiter, Hendricks had been beaten and prepared for his body to be absorbed into whatever crazy machine the alien had built for the purpose of sustaining the avatars. He came into contact with the ship's AI system and the other human consciousness, which it had been paired with. He had seen the ancient commander of the *Crimson Star* and had shared his memory of the disaster. The disaster had been total, and vast numbers of the population had died from lack of air, radiation, and freezing temperatures. There was massive loss of life in the habitat. He imagined, no, he knew that he must be travelling through a giant graveyard to reach the spot where the goddess had said he could find a tap to the ship's power. The weird illumination that was the desert at night made the whole experience an eerie one. Strange shadows seemed to crawl around him, their blackness so rich they almost seemed mauve.

After a time, the scattered stones ended, and he was able to climb back onto the horse. He came to a slim canyon, which seemed to go downward, an illusion perhaps of the elevation dropping as he moved farther west. Before he went into the canyon, he noted the Blue Mountains on the western horizon. They loomed over the wasteland like dark sentinels overlooking a grave.

Down he went into the canyon, and the shadows swallowed them up. He proceeded slowly as his eyes adjusted to the gloom. He was just beginning to relax when he heard it for the first time. Whispers, squeezing out of who knew where. Air flowed through the canyon, a breeze that picked up into a wind that seemed to catch the whispers, and they swirled around in the air, becoming more audible. They were horrid things to hear.

"No, no, no, nooooooo."

"Help us, help us—ahhhhhh, no, make it stop, no, no..."

Hendricks tried to cover his ears as he felt his body break into a sweat. Where were the voices coming from? He didn't believe in ghosts either, but this was giving him a fright just the same. He realized that Shep was hearing them too, as the horse picked up speed to get to the patch of light on the other side of the canyon. Suddenly, the illusions became visual as well; long, clawed hands burst through the ground, trying to grab or scratch the horse's legs. Hendricks struggled to control the panicking animal as it reared up, nearly throwing him to the ground.

Finally, they burst from the canyon with Shep at full gallop, going due west. More madness assaulted them then as the ground around them began to shake violently. The horse stopped suddenly and reared up again as a massive break in the ground opened up, creating a huge opening that ran north to south. Hendricks cursed madly as he fought with Shep to bring him under control. They swung around in the other direction and stopped short. A wall of rock and shale, a cliff that stretched up yards into the sky, now blocked their way. The horse snorted and shook his mane but began to calm now that he was forced to stop. Hendricks sat atop, staring in disbelief at the wall of stone.

This can't be happening, he thought. *It doesn't make any sense.*

"That wasn't there. A minute ago, that wasn't there," he muttered aloud. He slowly climbed down from the horse, still staring at the wall of rock. His mind was split between possibilities. *I've finally gone mad. Saturn has some power we don't understand. The world ship was breaking up somehow. No, I'm not buying in to any of that. Not after all I've seen lately, especially what the Auxconites could do with illusions. But would they have anything to do with this? They were our allies. Why would they interfere with my mission?*

Okay, so maybe not them, but they prove such illusions were possible, he thought angrily, *and I'm not buying into this illusion. It wasn't there a few moments ago. It wasn't there.*

Hendricks stood back from the wall and drew his sword. He didn't know what he was getting himself into here. Some kind of trap? He braced himself and then began to run toward the wall at a good speed. When he reached the right spot, he leaped into the air, shoulder out to protect him if he was wrong, or if he was right!

He flew straight at the wall of rock and then, with a gasp, went right through it. He was suspended in the air for a second, and then gravity did its trick. Hendricks fell hard onto the ground. He landed with a curse as everything seemed to flash.

"Goddamn it!" he cried out as the whole landscape changed. The wall was gone, the crevice from the earthquake was gone, and even the canyon he had ridden through was gone from the distance. It was all illusion. There was nothing there at all except Shep standing still and waiting for him, and the sound of the night wind rushing over the plain.

When day came in, he rested on a shallow outcropping of oddly formed rock. He was on the outskirts of a strange area of weird stone trees. That was what they looked like to him, anyway. Suddenly, he could see the landscape around him in a different way, as if he could see through the eyes of seven hundred years ago. He was indeed in the ruins of a transportation depot, the buildings crumbled and almost completely reclaimed by the environment; man-made perhaps, but this little world had a vivacious appetite.

It was a while before he could sleep, so he lay in a position of shelter where he could judge the sun of the day, and how long he had till sunset. He could not help but consider the illusions of the night before. This strange land of Terraroma got just a bit stranger with every year he was here. The Auxconites were the only ones who could do something like create the illusions he had seen the night before. *Are they not the allies that we believe them to be?* He thought of Denzeel, who had gone on a mission with Oniman. Had his friend walked into a trap? Somehow he believed that the Auxconites were on the level, insofar as they had no intention of doing harm to anyone. He respected their pacifist intentions and felt that this was a weakness, not realistic. Terraroma was a savage place.

Eventually, he drifted off and dreamed of the transportation depot, whole and alive and bustling with passengers. In the dream, he was waiting for a rapid rail, and it never showed up. He could see the rail car approaching through a window; it would grow close, then slip backwards. It never arrived.

After finally getting what sleep he could, Hendricks got up and ate some dried meat he'd brought along. He set out into the forest of stone trees, leading the horse as he went. After a short time, the "trees" began to spread out more and more until Hendricks saw a pattern. Soon, he saw a circular opening in a low ridge of stone up ahead.

My God! he thought suddenly. *I'm walking along the ruins of some type of track. It enters into that ridge there.* This was, in fact, the transportation system that he'd imagined; his dreaming self had recognized that this was the place he was looking for! This changed his mood entirely and it was almost a "whistle while you work" kind of a day.

In the end, it took Hendricks a lot longer to find the actual spot where the weapons could be recharged than he had anticipated. But finally, in the end, he prevailed. He'd been correct in thinking this was once some kind of transportation station. It was the ruins of one, and it had been a very long time since it was up and running. It was a depressing place to Hendricks because, to him, it was proof positive that they'd fallen through some kind of time warp. Vast centuries had passed here on this world ship, and he was now very far away from anything that he had ever known.

That was another life now. You know where and when you are right here and now, he told himself, *you grab hold of that and hang onto it, or you might as well be dead.* He thought of his Zingaris warriors; fierce and primitive, deadly. They were not the Miceenian army, but they were a force to contend with.

Then, as he waited, his thoughts turned to Jones. He had worried about how he would react to seeing her again. After all these years, she seemed exactly as she had been all those years ago. The only difference was now Hendrick could see the Jones he knew within the being that had been her broken body, now modified and recreated. The ghost in the machine.

After the last power pack was charged and stored away, Hendrick put his thoughts of the past away and began the journey back to the Zingaris. Whatever lay ahead of them all, he felt much more confident that he could handle it now.

16

DENZEEL AND ONIMAN IN NECROPOLIS

DENZEEL WAS ALWAYS amazed at how much faster it was to travel with just one companion than with a whole army or, in the case of the Zingaris, an entire town. As he and Oniman approached their destination of Necropolis, Denzeel considered how much things had changed over the last few years. He had travelled here with Hendricks and General Marcellus years ago when they'd made war upon the tyrant Magnus Jupiter. That journey had taken four solid weeks of marching; granted, they'd been slowed down by the attack from the hillmen. The very same hillmen that Brent was now working with.

Brent had left Miceen with half a legion of Miceenian soldiers. He was there at Hendricks's request; Brent seemed pretty horrified when the Tyrr told him he wanted him to travel north and work with the Gar-Tu as a kind of military adviser. Brent had argued that he couldn't advise anyone on how to run their army. "I'm a smuggler, not a general. What the hell could I tell them?" was about what he'd said, and it had made Denzeel laugh.

Hendrick tried to sound as sympathetic as he could, but was really just explaining what it was he wanted Brent to do—use the men from Miceen to try to get those savages organized beyond merely charging over a hilltop. *You can tell the difference between an army and a mob. Well, the Miceenians will help you, and you're there on my authority,* Hendricks had said to Brent. It had not been the first time that Brent had second-guessed Hendrick's orders. He could see how the pressures of leadership were weighing on the Tyrr, and Brent had thankfully let the issue drop.

That had been three weeks ago, and Denzeel had his own immediate concerns to deal with. He and Oniman had arrived at the newly named city of Necropolis that afternoon and were presently outside the walls of the city. After spending time on the road with this strange, robed man who barely seemed to speak and obviously had no sense of humour, Denzeel was glad to be getting down to business. There was nothing bad about the way Oniman behaved; he was polite and considerate, but he seemed to have no interests in common with Denzeel. It made for a long, dull journey.

Now Oniman would be called upon to get them into the city and find a safe place to hole up while they were spying on Saturn. The last time that he was here, Denzeel, Hendricks, and two other soldiers had broken into the city commando style. Not everyone made it back from that mission. Those were desperate days, and much was put at risk. People volunteered to put an end to the cycle of war that had been running rampant for many generations. That much, at least, had not changed.

Yet here they were again, lining up to go into battle, *So what has changed? Well, the players, for one thing.* Denzeel had grown to trust Hendricks like a brother and the respect was mutual. As he made his way across Terraroma, finding his destiny, Hendricks had brought Denzeel along with him and shared his success as they went. If Hendricks told him the danger had not yet passed from the land, then he would listen and follow his orders to the best of his ability.

Even outside of the city walls, Denzeel could see how the city, a place he once knew as Augustine (and had considered it wicked then), had changed even more so over the last few years. Although it was mid-afternoon and a bright day, Denzeel felt as if all the colour had been drained out of the city. It was an absurd thought to Denzeel, but it was more of a feeling than anything. The sounds of the city were different too, and this was not anyone's imagination. Indeed, the frenetic din of lightly controlled chaos that rose into the air was gone. Instead, there was a *crash bang boom* of things getting done with military efficiency. Denzeel wondered what it was like here after the sun line went into the dark hours.

They took a brief rest before approaching the walls of the city. Oniman had changed out of his monkish robes and now wore the more typical clothes of a city dweller. With the exception of his pale complexion, he now looked the part of a common worker or a merchant, perhaps. Denzeel took the time to hide away anything that he thought could connect him to the Zingaris or the Miceenians.

"Okay," said Oniman, "we're just going to walk right in the front gate. This is the easiest way to get inside without much interaction and of course without violence."

"You think we can avoid violence the whole time we're in this city?" Denzeel said to him with an admonishing smirk. "Have you any idea what has become of these people?"

"I have heard the testimony of the newly arrived friends. These are barbarians, I know. I have explained this before: we do not kill our enemies. We have lived this way for many years, and we find that, in time, the unrighteous destroy each other or themselves."

"I'm following the Tyrr's orders, and he said to trust your methods, so let's see what you can do," said Denzeel with a gesture of resignation.

Oniman signalled for him to follow as they approached the main gate, an ominous double door of wood and steel. He spoke quietly as they got closer. "Just walk up to the gate with me and do not speak, even if you think it's important. Just don't say anything. I am going to put suggestions into the minds of the several people behind the gate. If you speak at the wrong time or startle me, the illusion may be broken, and the guards may see us for who we really are."

"I can get in and out of the city without all this hocus pocus," Denzeel snarled under his breath.

Oniman gave Denzeel one more nasty glare and then picked up his pace as they came to the gate. Arrows appeared in the turrets high up on the walls. Denzeel had to fight back the instinct to draw his weapon. Someone looked out at them through a small slot in the gate.

"Halt, slaves!" a stern voice called out.

"It is only us, my friends. The grain merchants from southern Celphon," Oniman called up to them.

To Denzeel's surprise, the gates unlocked in short order, and a stout, mean-looking man came out as the doors opened wide.

"Maybe you'd be the wine merchants, huh?" the man said quickly, staring at Oniman. There was a hard moment where silence hung in the air like a vulture trying to decide whether it was safe to approach his prey. Then the tension broke as the guard leaned closer and spoke to Oniman in a low voice. "Those flagons that you boys set me up with last time were damn good. Come on in here quick." He swung a lever and the gate clanged shut again with Denzel and Oniman safely inside the city.

Five minutes later, they were strolling down the main road and away from the guard tower. Denzel wasn't surprised by the unhealthy quiet of the city. Oniman was poker-faced as usual, but Denzeel knew he must have noticed the atmosphere of fear that hung in the streets. The population knew to keep a low profile; they knew what happened to those who made too much of a commotion.

Within that first hour inside Necropolis, they secured a rented room. Oniman made sure the landlord had the overwhelming feeling that he should leave his new guests alone.

Denzeel had held his silence the entire time until they were safely behind a locked door, and then he spoke up to Oniman. "Very impressive, my friend. I just hope that no one comes looking for us once your little spell wears off."

"They are subtle thoughts that I plant in people's minds. The landlord, for example, fat brute that he is, doesn't even realize that he has any feeling about us at all. Should he try to think about us, he will be filled with a great feeling of dread. Better to ignore us," Oniman said with a small bow. "No blood."

Denzel nodded in agreement. They were safe enough for now.

***

The next day the pair got right down to the serious business of spying. They went to busy public areas, and both observed the activities going on and eavesdropped on several conversations. It quickly became obvious that the whole of the city of Necropolis was involved in preparing a large army for a long campaign. Large quantities of supplies—food, weapons, and other fortifications—were being organized. From what Denzeel could see, these were not defensive actions; they were not preparing to endure a siege or outright attack. This was an invasion force that was being mounted. They had underestimated the ambition and speed of this devil.

Denzeel felt his skin crawl. He and Oniman had come here to spy and perhaps learn the defence capabilities of the city, but they had found a war machine almost ready to go. There was no advantage to capitalize on here, only a sleeping serpent now coiled to strike! Would there be time enough to warn the Zingaris and their allies?

Denzel knew the armies in the south were likely on the move by now; the first battles would be struck on open land between the two major cities. They would not be able to stay in the city long, and Denzeel expressed his worry to Oniman that they could neither gather more intelligence nor warn the allies. Time. If only they had more time. Oniman was quick to point out that at least they had a chance to warn those in the south. Had they not come here, the surprise would have been complete.

On the third day in the city, they encountered a small group of soldiers who were preparing to ride ahead and scout for trouble. Denzeel wanted to go after them and perhaps kill them on the road. Oniman insisted that it was a fool's errand. They had abandoned the horses that they rode to the city, and it would take time to secure fresh ones and provisions for the return journey. Oniman insisted that Denzeel be patient. Denzeel, who hated inaction, grumbled but could not defeat his companion's logic.

On the fourth day, they learned of the special public gathering in the arena. This was the event that eventually forced them into action, and although the intelligence they gathered at the event was terrifying, Denzeel felt better that Oniman could see that they could wait no longer. They had to get on the road as soon as possible. Denzeel, who was incredibly uncomfortable inside the arena in plain sight, had a hard time containing himself during the event.

There were two specific points that came to light and unnerved the two spies.

First, there was the business of seeing Saturn's right hand. Partly by description and partly because of his odd dress and mannerisms, they realized that the Hand was in fact the third member of Brent's group, Simon. Denzeel knew the tale of how Brent had to cauterized Simon's arm when Saturn's soldiers cut it off. This was the same man, his hand now grown back to crazy proportions, and there he was, side by side with the very evil which they dreaded: Saturn himself.

Second, there was the introduction of the flying soldiers. This mystified Denzeel at first, but when he realized the kind of damage they could do from the air, he was terrified. There was dark magic at work here, to be sure. They had to get out of Necropolis.

After Saturn had made his speech calling for invasion, they made their way out of the arena. They did not even return to the rented room they'd shared there. They would get outside of the gates and then decide on plans. They moved through the streets quickly, securing perhaps a week's provisions each. Oniman, who was beginning to look a bit overtaxed, provided a couple of good horses for them by convincing a merchant that he owed the men two fresh horses.

This time, when they were at the city gates, they were stopped by guards who were being pretty officious. The Auxconite put the idea in the main guard's head that the two had already provided sufficient reasons to leave the city. Once they were at a safe distance, they rode hard, going south for an hour; Denzeel said nothing but cursed under his breath at the less experienced Oniman's lesser speed. Finally, they stopped to confer about the best plan of action.

They stopped after crossing to the far side of a bridge that covered a small tributary of the local river, Nix. This position brought them to a crossroads. Denzeel leaned over in his saddle, regaining his breath after the sprint away from Necropolis. Oniman drank water in gulps. They took a small path off the main road, and when they felt that they were in a visually safe place, they dismounted and rested for a short time.

"These are grim tidings indeed. The Tyrr must be warned," said Denzeel.

"And the Good Goddess and the Miceenian army!" Oniman added. Denzeel nodded in agreement and although unspoken, it was obvious that the pair would have to split up; this was the only hope of warning both parties of the coming danger. After some discussion and a quick survey of what provisions they had between the two of them, they decided that Denzeel would ride for the Zingaris, and Oniman would try for the Miceenian army. They rode back to the main road, and that was when they discovered, to their horror, that they had somehow been tracked from Necropolis.

A party of five Saturnian guardsmen galloped after them as soon as they made visual contact. They took off as fast as they could with the soldiers in pursuit.

"Do something!" Denzeel yelled to Oniman as they rode hard once again.

"I am fatigued," Oniman yelled back. "We are only men! I will try!"

They kept fifty yards away from the on coming threat, but it soon became obvious that the guardsmen were gaining on them.

Suddenly, with a great war cry, Denzeel swung his horse around and drew his sword, meaning to meet their enemies head-on. Oniman also turned to join him, although he himself had no weapon. When they had initially set out, Denzeel had warned Oniman that his pacifism would come to no good. That was, however, before he saw what the Auxconite was capable of.

The two groups were perhaps ten yards from each other when suddenly three of the five soldiers in pursuit began to scream and claw at the air, savagely trying fight off some illusion that Oniman had put in their heads. The other two still came on, seemingly unaffected by the Auxconite's attempts. One of the afflicted men fell from his horse and the other two rode erratically in no particular direction.

Denzeel came in close toward one of the two remaining men. He ducked below a swinging blade and struck out with his own weapon at the same time, easily running through the first man who went sprawling in a trail of blood. The second man charged at Denzeel and this time a blade grazed his left arm, drawing a superficial wound. Denzeel, a veteran of many campaigns, paid no heed and parried the second blow with ease. This time, Denzeel was able to slash at the man's torso and, after tottering upon the horse for a moment, the soldier fell from his horse, mortally wounded.

As Denzeel fought the two, Oniman continued his psychic assault on the others, who were all now off their mounts and battling unseen horrors. Once he had finished the two, Denzeel leaped from his horse and dispatched the three. He was quick, merciless, and savage.

Once it was over, Oniman stood and stared at the carnage in horror. "Was it really necessary to kill those three? We could have been gone before they recovered," he said flatly.

Denzeel stared at him in disbelief. He did not enjoy killing, but life had taught him that it was needed and to fear it was to sign one's own doom. He was angry and frustrated with this strange man once again, and he wished that Hendricks had not asked this mission of him. He walked over now and looked the Auxconite straight in the eye.

"Fuck you, Oniman," he said in a quiet voice. "You must drop this foolish attitude, or you will never reach the Miceenians alive." He walked away and as he did, the reply came at his back.

"This is not my world, you mad savage," Oniman said. "I am of the outer world. I am Auxconite, and we do not kill our enemies. We get our enemies to kill each other."

Denzeel gave out a grunt of disgust. He walked around the fallen soldiers and took whatever he found to be useful from them. There wasn't much; some extra water and a few weapons, in particular a knife with a very long and sharp blade.

The two rode away from the scene without speaking. They rode at a respectable speed until they came to another split in the road. This was where they would part ways. Denzeel was glad of the fact, although he wished no harm upon the man. As a matter of fact, he had been trying to think of some ways to help this fool achieve his mission. He looked at Oniman and attempted a smile. He rode closer to the Auxconite and tried to give him the long-bladed knife he had found.

"You don't have to plan to use it," Denzeel said. "Just keep it on you in case you need it."

Oniman merely looked at him as if he were trying to hand him a poisonous snake. "I think not," he said flatly. "Good luck to you, Denzeel, and safe journey." He turned his horse and began to ride away in the southern direction.

Denzeel watched Oniman riding away. He wondered if the fool would live to warn the Good Goddess of the threat of the flying soldiers. Well, he had tried to help the man. Who knew? The man was dangerous enough without a sword perhaps. After a moment's reflection, he hitched up his horse and rode east to find Hendricks and the Zingaris. To the north, dark clouds grew upon the horizon, and Denzeel picked up his speed.

17

WAR MARCH

AT THE SAME time that Denzeel and Oniman were having their spying adventure in Necropolis, Macy Jones—a.k.a. the Good Goddess of the Miceenian people—was riding at the front of the military procession that was marching on that same city. They had left the city limits of Miceen one week earlier, and it was the first time since becoming the Good Goddess that Jones had gone out into the greater environment of Terraroma. She had visited towns and villages close to the home city at the beginning of her reign as she began to appreciate the scope of the society she had taken control of, but this was the first long excursion.

Recent events had been difficult on the goddess, or at least the Macy Jones aspect of her. She had resigned herself to civilizing the population. That at least had helped to quell the despair she felt at having been absorbed into the Magnus 9 AI matrix that controlled the larger Terraroma environment. Her mind was forever splintered, and part of it was running purification systems and automated sun line maintenance protocols while she actually gazed out at the western horizon.

Looking west, the land lifted gently and far off, through lightly scattered cloud cover, green fading into a light sandalwood hue. How beautiful and strange these lands were. She knew that the Great Desert lay far off in the direction she was gazing but could not be seen. She had almost forgotten the mind-blowing vistas and the incredible size of the McKendree cylinder.

She hated what she was doing; she was leading her people into war after preaching peace for the last five years. Then again, she knew what the threat of Saturn was out there, and there would be no lasting peace until it was dealt with.

It seemed that the people trusted her implicitly, but she still hated the contradiction that came with her position. She remembered hearing similar rhetoric from politicians out in the Sol System for years even as she was employed as a military captain and thinking then that it was hypocrisy. To preach peace while preparing for war. Now it was she who was living the contradiction, and she considered that her judgment had been hasty; this dichotomy of the human species was perhaps more profound than she had realized. War was the only viable option in the face of such evil.

She could at least ensure good weather until they reached the Eastern Pass. She could, in fact, affect changes in the weather patterns; being part of the matrix that ran the cylinder's environment, she was able to reduce the cloud cover in the area where the army was marching. The winds within the pass were bringing the needed season changes to the south, and she would not play with that. It was a mandatory part of the lands and the cycles that kept them healthy.

The goddess wore a gold chest plate and a helmet with a crimson plume. She rode at the front of the thirteenth legion, and the thirteenth rode at the front of the Miceenian Third Army. They were a legend in Miceen, the thirteenth, with the toughest, most-talented veterans mixed with the strongest, most-promising new recruits. The army was opening up to a new generation now. When the war upon Saturn was declared, General Maximus Torus was demoted to the position of military adviser as the goddess announced that she herself would be the general to lead the Miceenian Third Army. *Put your money where your mouth is Jones*, she had told herself.

Jones marched the army hard; she knew that approximately 30 percent of the army were new soldiers who had never seen a real battle. If she couldn't have them blooded before the first battle, then she'd give them strong legs like tree trunks. She pushed them for a time each day, marching at a pace that was a jog, to say the least. Let them hate her now and love her later when the last battle was truly fought. She rode a horse she named Lightbringer, who was an Arabian charger, a magnificent animal that had not changed in millennia. The gold of her armour nearly matched the strange colour of her skin, and she looked like a gold statue atop Lightbringer, all gold except for the crimson plume.

Two and a half weeks into the march, they camped before the opening of the Eastern Pass, an area in the east of Terraroma where the land had survived great catastrophe and not been turned into desert. This was the only way north that did not involve crossing the Great Desert, a task which would prove unbearable for a large marching force. The pass was like a great green windy gully. A gully that stretched many miles across and many more north to south. Light rain lingered to the north of their camp, and the experienced soldiers began to close up tent flaps and tie down loose supplies; they knew the promise of weather change was a promise that was kept in Terraroma. There was little need for Jones to inform the people of incoming weather; she knew all the weather changes and environmental systems within the great cycle of Terraroma; indeed, she was the weather, in a sense.

The weather was becoming cooler now as the autumn harvest season was coming to the southern lands. The goddess looked out the flap of her war tent. The storm was now upon them and rolled out of the pass as heavier rain poured down on the camp.

The Good Goddess had assembled the centurions and commanders. Her military adviser was there also. One young centurion she knew as the grandson of a noble family in Miceen; he was Cais Xon, grandson of Hortensia Garis, and he rose quickly in the ranks, perhaps through connection and perhaps by ambition. She had originally been opposed to him receiving the rank of centurion when he had never seen a battle. He was young, and that was not a crime, and they had all believed that a long peace would hold after the fall of the avatars. She had let the matter go, and now there was no time to replace him. He was performing fine thus far. She addressed the assembled soldiers. She noted the perhaps 15 percent of the Miceenian army were female; such a mishmash of human triumphs and human failing, this Terraroma.

"Soldiers of Miceen, I welcome you, and I invite your participation as we prepare to meet the threat of Saturn. Before I open the floor, I have some directives to cover. This will be the last significant stop we make until we have cleared the Eastern Pass. Once we are in the Northlands, we will camp again and await a message from our allies," she said to them without much emphasis.

They continued to speak of particular logistical issues to which there was some discussion and ultimately, conclusions. When the process was finished, she opened the floor to new issues. There was only one. A commander by the name of Cruis Rex stood up and bowed to the Good Goddess, as was the custom before addressing her.

"Great one, I beg your patience, but it is my way to speak my mind," he said.

"Then do so!" Jones said to the man. Her Macy Jones aspect truly hated the extreme ass-kissing that went on, but her advisers insisted that the people wanted to do so.

"It would seem to me," Cruis continued, "that to stop at the bottom of the northlands would be an unwise strategy. Would it not be better to continue to march north for a time?"

"Perhaps, under different circumstances, that would be the prudent choice. However, our objective is a coordinated attack upon Necropolis and much depends on the exchange of intel ... uh, information in a timely manner," the goddess said. She looked out at the centurions to see if she detected any dissent. She saw none and continued.

"Besides that, there's one other matter to which I have not spoken of openly yet. We also await weapons that will give us a great advantage. I speak, of course, of the fire sticks which are legend of the last war."

A rumble went through the assembly, but it died down as she continued on. "Our ally from the wastelands, John Hendricks, the Tyrr of the Zingaris, has gone upon a mission to recharge, that is replenish with fire, the two weapons which we brought to Terraroma years ago. These weapons, of themselves, do not ensure our victory, but if used with wisdom, they will certainly tip the balance of power. They can be used to cleanse this world of the evil which haunts it!" She said the last sentence with more emotion than intended and banged the small desk before her.

The assembled gave an enthusiastic cheer to this, and Jones concluded that she had done her cheerleading act for the day.

"We disembark at dawn, then. A rest on the other side of the Eastern Pass."

The briefing broke up then, and the leaders went off to call for preparation for the next day's march. The rain came on for hours but let up before first light. The rain had brought with it cooler weather, and that was a simple fact. The brisker air picked up the pace of the camp, and when the advance was sounded, the Third Army was ready. The thirteenth legion, with the Good Goddess Macy Jones at the lead, led the Third Army of Miceen into the Eastern Pass.

18

FURY IN THE NORTHLANDS

BRENT HAD ALWAYS thought that he had seen a fair amount of violence in his life, but after today, he would realize he didn't know what violence was. Standing back to back with Gar-Tu, he was covered with sweat from his hard work and blood from both himself and the enemies he had dispatched. The bodies of several dead soldiers of Necropolis lay about him. Behind him, Gar-Tu grunted as he smashed the life out of the last of the attackers. All around him, he could see both hillmen and the legion of Miceenian soldiers walking through the battlefield, stepping around gore and fire to search for wounded comrades or enemy survivors. The battle was over at last. The air was thick with the smell of smoke and blood; it burnt Brent's nostrils.

He leaned heavily on his sword for support. He looked at the field around him as the adrenalin drained from him, and he felt the wound in his thigh more acutely. After the Great Council, he and Gar-Tu had marched north with one legion of the Miceenian army. They had just arrived at the decided spot to meet with a larger group of hillmen and had been set upon on the second day. A large contingent of Saturn's soldiers had surprised them, and they had fought hard and defensively for nearly three hours until, at last, their friends finally arrived. Hundreds of hillmen came pouring onto the battlefield, and the Necropolis soldiers were now suddenly on the defensive. The Miceenian legion had regrouped then and tore back into the enemy. The end result lay all around him, a landscape of the dead. A great many hillmen and Miceenians had paid with their lives, but they had been the total victors of the battle.

Gar-Tu walked off, barking orders and greeting some of the new arrivals.

Using his sword like a cane, Brent limped over to where Centurion Marius Dane sat with a medic. He sat down hard beside Dane, who gasped when he saw Brent's leg wound. The Miceenian insisted the medic see to Brent immediately, and when Brent protested, he would have none of it.

"May the Good Goddess damn their eyes to hell!" the centurion said sternly. "We didn't see that coming until it was too late, and that is on us, but gods, those bastards were evil. They had a sick way about them, is what I mean." He shook his head; blood had dried on his left cheek. Dane was a tall, slim man by Terraroma standards, with a dark complexion and light brown hair. Like many people within the cylinder, his genealogy was impossible to guess; a mishmash of all the peoples of earth's history.

"Yes, there is something wrong with them; it's as if Saturn is bringing out the worst in his people." Brent had seen some of life inside Necropolis, however fleeting his captivity had been, but it seemed to him that Saturn would reward the most daring, the most ruthless, and the cruellest of his people. He turned vice into virtue, a real hard-core gangster. The attacking soldiers and been real maniacs, to be sure, and possessed of an almost hateful glee. Blood lust burnt in their eyes like a candle in an empty room; they were hell-bound on killing their enemies and nothing else.

Brent and Dane had spoken at length over the past weeks about the mission ahead of them: to work with the hillmen and teach them military tactics and skills that would be effective against the likes of Saturn's forces. Easier said than done, this task that had been given to them by the council. One goal was to try to get the hillmen to form some type of cavalry. The hillmen did not use horses as of yet, although there were plenty of horses in Terraroma. The Gar-Tu had been taught how to ride coyotozen in the past, by Magnus Jupiter, Hendricks had told Brent when he was briefing him for the mission. That, however, would require some technical access to the carrion eating machines and Brent had none. Still, the logic went if they could ride those things then horses couldn't be too hard.

The sudden ambush had made Brent think twice about this task; perhaps it was better to try to work with the hillmen's existing strengths. Fighting on horseback wasn't Brent's strong suit; he still couldn't believe he was actually riding around on one on a daily basis.

It surprised him how fast he was adapting to this odd, primitive lifestyle. Truth was, Brent felt better than he had in years. He was stronger, healthier, and here in Terraroma, he was respected by the people in his life. Back home, he was a criminal who made his living working around the system. Here he was able to play a larger role, and his opinion was valued. Hendricks had recognized leadership skills in Brent that he himself had been oblivious to.

Brent winced as the medic applied some limp, dark green leaves to his leg wound. The leaves would help fight any infection, he was told by the medic, a boy of perhaps seventeen with coarse dark hair and sympathetic eyes.

"We could waste a lot of time trying to get these guys up on horseback," Brent said to Dane. "From what I saw today, these hillmen have the capacity for strategy tactics. I'm thinking of how they held back men up on that hill. When the Necropolis soldiers tried to retreat, that group fell on them and mopped the ground with them."

"They're fierce, I'll say that. and they fight to the death," Dane said.

"What do you think we could teach them? Forget about this extra cavalry business. What then?"

Dane thought about it for a moment, then let out a long sigh before speaking. "With all respect, Mr. Brent, I know that the Good Goddess has told us to respect you as we would her, and I don't mean to second-guess your orders, but I have to wonder if teaching them anything is a good idea. I know a tactic that we could teach them, but I have to wonder if we might regret it later. In fact, this is one of the tactics that has worked very well *against them*. Any veteran of the Miceenian army will tell you, the best way to fight hillmen is to tire them out first, then you have the advantage."

"Well?" Brent asked. "Get to the point, man."

"What happens if we train them in straightforward Miceenian military tactics and someday in the future, long after this crisis had passed, the Gar-Tu fight against us and use the tactics we taught them?"

He sighed. "I guess we don't have much choice here. Okay, we can get started in the morning and I'll show you what I mean then. It'll be easier." Captain Dane stood and gave Brent a very loose salute.

"All right, tomorrow morning then," Brent said with a tired frown. He'd had quite enough for one day.

When the next day rolled around, and the group was resettled a kilometre away from the battlefield that was their old camp, Brent went out to oversee the training of the hillmen. His wounded leg was stiff but fully functional when he got moving that morning. He had spoken to Gar-Tu, who made sure that the first group of hillmen was ready for training. The hillmen had been roaring drunk the night after the battle, as was their tradition, but were up and ready when the assembly was called. Smoke from the burning pyres of the dead clouded the horizon, and the smell on the breeze was nasty.

Two groups were organized for a battle drill to demonstrate the new tactic. The first group was merely set into one large group while the second was set in a battle square, six across and six deep. At the back of the second group, their captain stood and waited while the two groups engaged. On his signal, the first six at the front of the second group dropped back, and six new soldiers came forward; it became obvious after a time that the first group was becoming tired out and the second group, giving their men a chance to rest and catch their breath, was still fresh well into the exercise.

Brent was impressed and could see the merit of the demonstration; to simply try to explain it to the hillmen would have been a waste of time. He, himself, had little military knowledge and certainly not for the type of ancient ground battles that were taking place in this bizarre world. Hendricks had explained that the Miceenians were well acquainted with war and had several hundred years of practice at refining their tactics. Brent could see that this was quite true.

After about a week of training, Brent was happy to note that the hillmen were making great progress. They would soon be a fighting force to contend with. He also noticed that several soldiers were not happy about sharing this fighting knowledge with the Gar-Tu, just as Dane had said. Brent came to understand that they feared that someday they would face the hillmen in battle. They'd always known the northerners as enemies, not allies, and now the hillmen could use these same tactics against them. It was a reasonable concern and exactly the type of issue that Hendricks and the Good Goddess wanted Brent to quell.

"What do you think your Good Goddess would say about all this?" Brent had asked a young soldier one evening as they all shared some ale.

"Oh, she would say that this was blasphemy and that we needed to see peace as the way of the future, once this evil is destroyed, that is," the soldier said, looking a bit abashed. He wanted to say more, but he knew better than to contradict someone of higher rank. "What do you think, Mr. Brent?" he added.

"Oh, shit, I don't know," Brent replied. "I think peace is a great thing to work for. As far as I can see, humans have always made war upon each other. So, what can you say? People used to believe that when we became capable of going beyond our home world that all the wars would stop once and for all." Brent could see that the soldier wasn't following what he was saying.

He reminded himself that they knew nothing of space travel here, and he should watch what he says about such things. He thought about the whole tale that Hendricks had told him about how the *Crimson Star* had become the way it was now, that and the bizarre time warp they'd all gone through. They were all deep in the future now. Hundreds of years had passed for *Crimson Star* while he and the others who came from outside simply jumped ahead. He had no idea what they would find if they escaped back to their own place in the solar system. Would the time warp reverse, or would they find a reality that they didn't know, a civilization hundreds of years ahead of them?

Brent realized the soldier was staring at him as his mind wandered.

"Well, I've seen Saturn up close and personal," Brent said, "and I agree that he should be stopped. If Saturn gains dominion, he'll enslave all the free people of Terraroma. What hope of peace if that happens?"

The soldier merely grunted and drank down his ale. A loud belch followed, and the soldier laughed.

Brent smiled, but he groaned inwardly. *Welcome to my new reality*, he thought.

One day during a late-afternoon training session, their routine was shattered as a soldier came and cried out to the captain and group alike. "Lone rider approaching! He's riding in like the wind!"

Centurion Dane called a recess. He and Brent moved quickly across the camp to the eastern guard post, where makeshift walls had been constructed. This was a classic Roman adaption that had been in use as long as the Miceenians could remember; each night, the company would camp, and a solid perimeter of wood was thrown up and torn down as needed. The organizational skills alone were impressive. Brent saw that soldiers were going outside with weapons drawn.

Dane jumped up onto the guard post and called down to the soldiers. "At ease, you men there. He is a single rider. You archers stay sharp, though. Let's see what this is."

Brent climbed up to where Dane was so he could get a better view of the approaching rider. The landscape was gently rolling grasslands, and a haze mixed with the glaring sun line made visibility difficult. The rider was much closer now, and all could see that he rode like a man with hell on his heels. Brent wondered if the man was being chased, but there appeared to be no one behind him.

The horse slowed but did not stop as it came up to the gates. "Open the gates, I say. I bring news of the war! Open the gates!" the man called out.

Dane nodded to the soldiers below, and the gate was opened. The man rode in, and froth fell from his exhausted steed. The rider, wearing a hood and cloak, wavered atop the horse. Brent thought for a moment that the man would fall right off his mount. He did not, but seemed uneasy as he climbed off the horse.

As Brent came down to where the rider was, he heard him speaking but could not see him in the gathering dusk.

"I must get word to the Tyrr of the Zingaris. Saturn's forces are on the move right now! We are too late to contain them within their city!" the man said. He was of medium height with a wiry build, and then Brent realized who this person was. It was Denzeel who was Hendricks' second in command with the Zingaris! Brent rushed over and clapped him on the shoulder. Denzeel looked exhausted, and dark circles were under his bloodshot eyes.

"Denzeel, what happened to you out there? Where is Oniman?" Brent said to him.

"Mr. Brent, it is good to see you," Denzeel said and then went slack jawed. Suddenly his knees buckled, and he went down. Brent tried to grab him but missed, and Denzeel collapsed into a heap at their feet. He had passed out from exhaustion.

Denzeel was taken to a tent and seen to by the same medic who had helped Brent some days before. Brent and Captain Dane waited until they were told Denzeel had regained consciousness and could talk to the brass, as it were. When they came into the tent, Denzeel was trying to get up from the cot he was on.

"At easy," Dane said. "You can talk fine from where you are." The medic had said Denzeel should rest for a few days before doing anything much. Denzeel had said that wasn't possible, and then Centurion Dane had stepped in and ordered him to rest for two days. Denzeel wasn't answerable to Dane or anyone from Miceen, but he agreed anyway, either because he saw the sense of it or because he was respecting Dane as being in command there. Denzeel sat on the cot and looked up at the two men in the tent with him.

"The devil of the north is already on the move. We split up, I to find the Tyrr and Oniman went to warn the goddess and the Miceenians. They march south even now, and they are armed with dark magic!" Denzeel said. He paused briefly, as if collecting his words before continuing. "All our fears were confirmed when I reached Necropolis. With Oniman's tricks, we were able to spy within the city, and it is an evil and unhealthy place now."

He looked at Brent then, as if recalling something. He went on. "Brent! We saw the other man who came with you, Simon. It had to be he ... his hand. He is alive, and he serves Saturn now."

Brent stared for a moment. "What?"

"He has gone mad or become evil or both, I tell you," Denzeel continued. "He has been changed, somehow. Saturn has grown his missing hand back, and it is horrible. Big, too big, and ugly, hairy with great nails! And that is not the worst; there is dark magic at work. They have soldiers that can fly."

"Come on now," said Centurion Dane. "Are you feeling yourself? No soldier or anyone, for that matter, can fly." He stared at Denzeel now, wondering if the man had been hallucinating, suffering from his mad ride. He looked over at Brent, who was also looking at Denzeel intently.

After a moment, Brent broke into the issue. "Maybe not," he said. "Denzeel, tell me more of these flying soldiers. How is it that they fly? Do they have wings?"

"No, of course not!" Denzeel said angrily. "It is true, Brent, I do not lie, and I am not mad. Oniman saw this also. They fly like gulls in great swoops, like giant kites in a high wind!"

"Like a glider!" Brent said, sounding astonished.

"What is a glider?" Dane said.

Brent held his hand up as he was thinking about something. He had seen things like this on Mars, at a resort where people went up high to the top of the domed hotel. The lighter g made it easy and safer than it would be on Earth, but he understood people did this on the oceans on Earth as well.

"We learned that man, Simon, who came here with you and who they now call the Hand, took men up into the mountains and developed this dark art," Denzeel added.

"The mountains. Of course!" Brent said suddenly. "The closer to the centre of this world you go, the g would get lighter. You could really fly a hang glider up there, if that's what they have."

Well, that's a hell of a twist, Brent thought. He began to consider the implications of the other side having some kind of air assault. But what? A bow and arrows wouldn't work well in a glider. Even if a soldier could master such a thing, the accuracy would be bad. "This isn't good at all but thank God you and Oniman got out in time to warn us. I can only assume that the goddess will know how to deal with this new threat."

"Will Oniman reach them in time, Saturn's legions having the element of surprise?"

Denzeel groaned a bit and shifted his position on the cot. The mere thought of his odd companion gave him pause. "I cannot say for certain. He will not be riding as I was. It was a wonder the man stayed up on his horse at all. We left quickly enough to get at least a day ahead of the army that was massing to march south."

"How big is the force that marches south?" Dane asked quickly.

"I am guessing, but from what we saw, I would say 50,000 soldiers."

Captain Dane looked up from Denzeel and spoke directly to Brent. "There is much to consider and little time to do so. The Good Goddess marched with an army of 30,000. The Zingaris have 10,000, and perhaps more. The hillmen have 20 to 30 thousand, so we have the numbers. Do we head for Necropolis now or stick to the plan of meeting up with the goddess and the Miceenians?"

"They have more, perhaps a whole other army. Saturn would not leave the city undefended," Denzeel said.

Then a herald came to tell the centurion that many were approaching from the east. Dane excused himself in short order.

Brent wondered what was coming and he saw Denzeel beaming.

"It must be Hendricks and the Zingaris," he said.

Brent had to stop him as he tried to get up again, obviously intent on giving his report to the Tyrr.

And it was, indeed, Hendricks and the Zingaris.

19

THE BATTLE OF THE EASTERN PASS

THE MICEENIAN ARMY was camped at the northern passage, which led up out of the Eastern Pass. To the west of the camp were slowly rising hills that gave way to distant grasslands. To the south, the way they had come, the land faded into darkness. To the north, an ancient road led uphill out of the mouth of the Eastern Pass Finally, to the east, which held one of the oddest sights in Terraroma. As the land slowly led away, it curved upward until the peaks of the Blue Mountains pointed down from the far east at what looked to be a bit less than a 45-degree angle.

They had been there for two nights, awaiting the arrival of their allies and planning the siege of Necropolis. This was not an unexpected respite in the campaign; Macy Jones knew the possible reason for a delay. She assumed that Hendricks had completed his mission into the northern badlands and that he and his Zingaris had been riding almost constantly to make the rendezvous in a timely fashion. Things happen on the road, and Hendricks would travel some strange roads up in the badlands; delays were inevitable. She felt certain that they would arrive soon.

Her army was efficient and ready to march on Saturn and his forces as they would ever be. Jones had called for a period of rest to reward the soldiers's hard work and their long march. Great barrels of ale were brought out, and the second night was filled with songs and revelry. The Miceenian army was approximately 20 percent women, and the great imbalance in the genders had caused Jones to give the order that all soldiers refrain from sex. She wasn't really sure why she did this;

the Miceenians were a very sexually mature people, and there was no prejudice regarding orientation. This wasn't some barracks on Mars. There would be a few rebels who would go ahead anyway after enough ale got going, but there would be no trouble. She knew her people.

After watching the revelry from a position of some privacy, she noticed that the party was winding down and let her complex mind begin to multitask in other areas of the world. There was the problem of overriding the weather system for a short time; every time that she did so, the main system would begin repairing what she had just done. Right now, she wanted heavy cloud cover over Necropolis so that they could attack at night with the advantage of darkness. It was just as well, she supposed. The weather systems had been running smoothly for hundreds of years and no permanent changes were advisable. Jones no longer slept; she needed to have a rest period once a day and occasionally used a special interface with the matrix to reboot her electronic molecular systems. She was watching the party and sometimes smiling at the action. Part of her mind, however, was in the main weather system, cracking a code. Her mind split again as the apparition of Vokova came to her, asking what she was doing,

Jones explained. "I wish to use all the means at my disposal now to rid this world of Saturn, of the alien. This isn't finished, not until that thing is purged from this world forever."

Vokova looked at her and she thought that he wore a pained expression. A thought flashed across her neural interface. *Something strange in the northeast. Pay attention to this.*

Jones closed off her link to the matrix as best she could. She was always connected but could only focus on one aspect at a time. In this case, she was focused completely on her golden-skinned avatar; the Good Goddess, leader of the people of Miceen. She took note of the scene as a sudden feeling of tension and dread came over her. Dawn had come- and a few men and women moved around the camp doing early morning chores or heading off to their posting. The sky grew slightly brighter, and Jones looked around in every direction before stopping to look more intently to the northeast.

At first, she saw nothing unusual about the sky. It was a shell-coloured sky, which faded into brown as her gaze lowered. She could see the distant mountains pointing toward her position at 45 degrees. Then she suddenly noticed there was something like flies moving in the air much closer to the camp's position. They grew larger in the hazy sunlight until they looked like birds. Soon, she could tell that they were certainly not birds by the way they swooped and dipped up and down. Jones watched, almost mesmerized until she realized they were hang gliders of a type.

One flyer came close enough to reveal what they were: soldiers strapped into the oddest makeshift gliders, flying toward them, using the lighter g of the centre of the cylinder to pinpoint their attack. There were twelve in total as far as she could see.

She jumped up from where she had been resting and called out in her strong, thundering voice, "Alert! Alert! At attention, Miceenians. We are under attack!"

The camp exploded into a flurry of activity. Soldiers came to attention immediately while others stumbled about half asleep. Some were fast and some were slow and hungover, but they tried to form up as fast as possible. Some were not properly armoured up for battle but stood at the ready, boots on the ground, swords in hand.

That was the moment when the attack came, and the battle of the Eastern Pass began. The gliders swooped down and then back up again in random order. They began to drop again, but this time they dropped small payloads into the camp. The first one looked like a small package, but it exploded on impact, wounding two soldiers with shrapnel and causing a tent to burst into flames. This bizarre airstrike was something that had never been seen in Terraroma before; the camp was in chaos as more of the makeshift bombs exploded all over the camp.

Jones leaped up onto the back of a wagon and began to shout orders at once. She wondered about the introduction of bombs in Terraroma and thought about the principle of air superiority when she heard the battle horns. Jones looked out beyond the camp to the north and saw to her horror that a sizable cavalry was pounding toward them. They had only minutes before the real fighting began. They had been caught off guard on the lowland within the Eastern Pass exactly as she had been warned they might.

Thunder ripped through the air as one late bomb hit the guardhouse facing the north road. Saturn's cavalry hit the north end of the camp and broke through their defences in no time at all. The Miceenians gathered ranks and pushed back as hard as they could, but they were fighting in a defensive stance.

Infantry came swarming in behind the cavalry and the campsite turned red. Steel crashed into steel, and curses and cries filled the air as the morning grew brighter.

Jones, who had been directing soldiers into place, suddenly realized that the bombing had stopped. She assumed that they couldn't carry much payload A very skilled archer named Severius had brought down one of the gliders, and Jones saw the wreckage of the glider and a thin man with an arrow in his heart.

She quickly found her sword and her mount and rode toward the thick of the battle at the north end of the camp. This was Macy Jones acting as she would, forgetting the bizarre reality of her existence. When the enemy soldiers saw her, they rallied and tried to overwhelm her with numbers. She was the general and should have stayed back to direct the army out of this mess. Well, she had other problems on her right now,

Three men moved in on her position, two on foot and one on horseback as she was. One rider directed the other to flank Jones as he charged.

However, the Good Goddess of Miceen had a few tricks up her sleeve, as they were about to find out. At the time of her transformation, Jones had been wearing a military-grade armband, an amazing piece of military tech. It could act as a shield or a taser as she wished. It also gave her superhuman strength in that arm. It was wetware that was connected to her mind. Now, since her transformation, the armband was literally part of her and couldn't be removed.

The rider made his move and charged at Jones. Jones held her place as he came at her. The first man attacked from her right and she spun the horse around and came around swinging her large bronze sword. The blade was long and slightly curved at the top like a scimitar. She had a longer reach than most and the attacker's head flew from his shoulders.

Still in motion, she met the attacker on horseback; their blades clashed as he passed, and the last man came in to try his luck. Jones grabbed his swinging blade with her advanced arm and stopped it cold. She hung on as the amazed man tried to pull his sword free. Jones used the taser effect, and the shock went down the blade, jolting the man hard and sending him sprawling backwards.

The horseman came around again, charging fast. Jones had two swords now, and she prepared herself. She gripped the horse tight with her legs and crossed her arms, a sword in each hand. As the horseman attacked again, Jones swung her arms apart. One blade blocked his attack and the second beheaded him in short order. Jones took up the reins again and rode back out of the fray to a safer position.

She saw that the assault was coming in from three sides now. The only open way was back down deeper into the pass, and that wasn't an option; they would have to fight here. This was what she had been warned about; the possibility of being pinned down on the lowland road. She rallied her centurions and sent out orders.

The Miceenians formed up again and pushed back against Saturn's army; they fought them off their flanks and tried to make it up the road onto higher ground. After fighting into the early afternoon, Jones and her forces had battled their way onto the upper road.

Then the gliders returned, and chaos ensued as their front ranks were literally bombed. There were dead everywhere now, and Jones cursed under her breath. Her army was being slaughtered before the planned campaign even began. They fought for another two hours and found themselves back approximately where they'd started in the morning.

As the late afternoon set in, Jones became very restless and could no longer sit and watch, directing men to their death. With a cry, she drew her sword and rode into the fray once more. She killed as quickly and efficiently as she could; she hated this in many ways but she hated seeing her army destroyed even more. Jones had always had a contradiction in her personality, even before the Good Goddess event. She was a soldier, and she could kill, but she needed a good reason to fight. Something to believe in.

She rode directly into the heat of the battle, her military armband fully deployed, and her sword held high. She struck at the horsemen before her, fighting with such intensity that for a few minutes, she believed that she might actually turn the battle around. But it was folly. Her brave comrades were not faring as well as she. Her soldiers were dying all around her as quickly as she was dispatching her enemies. She looked at the situation more realistically now.

Now she found herself in the middle of a disaster. If her army fell here, Saturn would go on to march on Miceen rather than her army on Necropolis. As the light of day grew weaker, there was a lull in the battle; 50 yards lay between the armed lines and the no man's land in between was littered with corpses. Jones was quite sure that Saturn himself, the man who was once Marcellus, was not here at this battle.

During the last bombing, she had seen this other one, who was obviously in command. He was far back in the battle. She saw the banner of the legion he commanded; it showed a big stylized red fist on it, and if she understood the words from this distance, it read, "The Hand of Saturn." He was the ranking officer on the field.

Jones noticed the man himself directing soldiers into an area immediately following a bomb strike. There were two things about the man which made him stand out from the others. First was that his right hand was grotesquely proportioned, huge and hairy with sharp black nails. The second was his clothing; while he wore some armour, the rest of his attire was rather ragged spacer's clothing. This was the other man in Brent's party who had been captured by Saturn, Simon. Clearly, the man has gone mad and joined with the fiend. What had Saturn done to deform him so?

Jones wondered if the gliders would be back again before the darkness came. Surely, they couldn't do those bombing runs in the dark? With the great blast of a horn, Saturn's army charged at Jones's position once again. The lines clashed against each other again, and before long, the gliders reappeared again. This time, Jones despaired in her heart; she worried that they would be defeated here. Then, as the first bomb fell, salvation flashed on the horizon.

Light that wasn't from firelight and had a green tinge caught her attention, and she did not recognize the source at once. Then, as she watched, she realized what she was looking at, and she would have laughed had the situation not been so grim. It was from a laser weapon! Had she been here so long that she, once a soldier of the system, didn't recognize laser fire? It was Hendricks. It had to be!

As if to confirm her thought, another flash darted into the air, and one of the gliders burst into flame in mid-dive. Then another went up, and this time, the laser fire ignited whatever payload it carried, and the whole thing exploded.

Suddenly encouraged, Jones rallied several warriors, who began to hack a path toward the laser fire. She could hear cries of fear and astonishment rising from the new battle front. After several more minutes of fighting, she saw that the Saturnian fighters on the eastern flank were beginning to retreat. The enemy to the west was now suddenly trapped between her Miceenian legions and the new allies attacking in the north. Jones reined in her horse and her desire to join with Hendricks and the new front, and she turned and rode back toward the ruins of their camp. Her soldiers had the situation under control.

Green fire flashed more brightly as it was fully dark out now. The tide had turned. Jones could almost feel the spirits of the soldiers rising as they pursued Saturn's frustrated fighters. With an hour of the arrival of Hendricks and the allies, the Saturnian army was smashed where they fought. Many of the force, including the Hand, went into full retreat early in the counter-assault and escaped to the northeast toward the top of the Blue Mountain range.

The power of superior technology—that, and the sudden element of surprise—had saved the day in the end. Needless to say, however, Jones did not feel like celebrating.

The battle of the Eastern Pass was over.

20

THE DAMAGE DONE

HENDRICKS RODE THROUGH the carnage of the battlefield feeling a strange range of emotions; astonished, disgusted, exhausted, victorious. His horse moved slowly as Hendricks looked for Jones. The laser rifle was slung over his back, and he stared dumbly at the gory nightmare that lay all around. The group of allied forces had come upon the battle in progress, and Hendricks had ridden ahead of the bulk of the assembled armies by maybe 100 yards. He came galloping in and actually burnt a hole through their ranks.

Then he saw the gliders that were reported of from Denzeel's recon mission. He shot two of them out of the early evening sky and then proceeded forward to do battle with the Saturnian forces. He suddenly wondered how many he'd killed that day and was sickened by the thought. He drove it from his mind.

He saw a large tent, half-broken but still standing in the distance up ahead. A familiar flash of gold moved in front of it, and he knew that he had found Jones. Several of the wounded soldiers were assembled near the tent, which was being used as medical triage. Many lay on rolls on the earth; others were on stretchers. Others again walked around with bandaged heads and arms. Blood tinged the air of the scattered ruins of the Miceenian camp. Hendricks easily guessed that they had been openly attacked without warning.

He raised his hand in greeting as he approached the Good Goddess. Jones was a sight, her gold armour splashed with blood. The red plume of her helmet sat at her left leg and seemed to match the blood. Blood and gold swam in his vision for a moment.

"Greetings, Macy Jones," he said flatly.

She raised her hand in return. "What a disaster this was."

"The first group has started going north to strike a new campground. How long do you think you'll need to deal with the wounded and such?" he asked.

"I don't know yet," she said with a great sigh. "I'll have some real numbers by morning. Some of these people are going home. They have done their part for now."

"Of course," Hendricks said. He was surprised to find that the Good Goddess was more like the Macy Jones that he knew. Outlandish appearance aside, she was taller now and shone like a brick of gold, but the voice speaking to him was much more Jones-like than it had been during the Great Council. He considered trying to reason with her the way he might have years ago and then changed his mind. "Do you need anything from us immediately?" he asked.

"Well, perhaps a cohort of soldiers to help us with the wounded," she replied. "We are carrying a type of antibiotic that I discovered the Miceenians had all along but didn't really know how it worked. You and the others are welcome to some; it helps to prevent infections from the types of wounds soldiers suffer in this kind of warfare."

"That would be good," Hendricks said. "We didn't lose the kind of numbers that you did, but there were some nasty wounds I observed. The new camp will be well out of the lowlands of the pass. Join us when you can."

"Yes, we certainly need to modify our plans. A meeting of the leaders would certainly be in order," Jones said in a voice that sounded strained.

Hendricks reached into a saddlebag and drew out the laser pistol. He handed the weapon along with three charge packs to Jones, and she took them silently.

She gave Hendricks something like a smile and simply said, "This was exactly what I was trying to avoid. It was a pure massacre. I should have listened to the advice I was given. Now I want to hear what the other leaders, including you, have to say."

"All right, I'll see to things, and we can all meet soon." He could see how hard she was taking the losses, and he added, "You held the line, Jones. That's all anyone could have done in your situation."

The Good Goddess of Miceen looked at him and simply scowled in a very Macy Jones way. She said nothing.

Hendrick then turned his horse around and rode back toward his own camp. As he left, he looked around again and truly took in the scale of the battle and the damage. The camp itself was the very centre of the battlefield. He saw soldiers, some of them wounded themselves, tending to the dead bodies. The Miceenians separated the dead, their own soldiers and the enemy. Their dead would be burnt in a ceremony. The Necropoline dead would be left for the coyotozen, strange, ancient Von Neumann creations that still functioned, recycling biomatter for the world ship. Tomorrow night they would come and devour the dead.

He wondered if Jones would prefer to burn all the bodies. She was at least partly running things all over the world ship, including the coyotozen. Traditions, he figured that the Miceenians would be pissed if the enemy were given the honour of cremation. Damned superstitious humans.

By the end of the next day, all the nasty business of mopping up your army after it gets hammered was done. The Miceenian army joined the larger camp, where all the forces were now rallied. The fifth legion, which had been training the Gar-Tu before now, rejoined the larger army and Jones was glad for the additional numbers. Brent had moved over to the Zingaris side of the camp once the Desert Wolves were settled. Tomorrow they would plan the next step, but that night was a chance to catch their breath and reconnect with friends.

Hendricks and Helen held a small dinner in the Tyrr's private tent. Brent and Denzeel joined them there. Jones had been invited but declined the invitation, saying that she still had many things which demanded her attention.

"Well, look at you, Mr. Brent," Hendricks said with a grin and a wink at Denzeel. "Life among the Gar-Tu seems to agree with you. You look, well, tougher now."

"I don't know about that," Brent replied, "but they are some hard people these Gar-Tu. Exactly who you need at your back if you're in a fight. The idea of giving quarter or surrendering is simply not in their culture."

Helen shook her head upon hearing this and said to Denzeel, "And what of this Oniman? Where is he?"

"We just don't know. He was supposed to have been headed straight to the Good Goddess and warn her of the incoming assault. And those cursed flying things," Denzeel said. "I simply can't believe that he is dead. He was very resourceful in Necropolis. Some of the things he could do were amazing. But in the end, what was it worth if he couldn't deliver the intelligence in time?"

"Do you think he was killed by the enemy?" Brent said.

Hendricks came over closer to where the others were talking. His expression grim, he held the palms of his hands out in a gesture of openness and began to speak. "It was I who pushed for the Auxconites to be included. The sudden appearance of these people was a shock to all of Terraroma, to be sure. I made the assumption that they would be trustworthy allies. Was I wrong? We have no way of contacting Oniman's people."

"Maybe Saturn's men killed him," Brent said. "They have a camp in the Blue Mountains, the bastards. That's where they launch these big gliders from."

"This is dark sorcery, to be sure," said Denzeel. "The most evil of people are the ones who thrive in Necropolis now."

"Well, there will be plenty of time to speak of these matters in a council tomorrow," Hendricks said and gestured over to a table that had been set with the best of what the Zingaris had to offer. The nomads were masters of living in as much comfort as possible while being in constant travel. In the time since he and Denzeel had been among them, Hendricks had never seen them stop in one place for longer than approximately one month. They raised livestock as they went and acquired other goods as needed on the road. Dried meats, grains, and even fruits, some dried and some fresh, were arranged in a banquet that made one hungry just looking at the spread.

In addition to the meal, a special warm beverage called chunga was served; it was stronger than any other brew in Terraroma and had a sweet aroma. The trick with chunga was to drink it down at once through a straw before it cooled down. Helen remarked that the drink must have had its origins in Tibet on Earth, where something similar had been around for many centuries.

The rest of the evening passed about as pleasantly as it could under the circumstances, and everyone was happily full and a bit dizzy from the warm liquor.

The next day, an hour past noon, the leaders of each of the factions, along with their advisers, met to discuss plans for the next stage of the war. Jones, dressed in a simple army-issue uniform, began the talks by thanking the Zingaris and the Gar-Tu for coming to their rescue at the top of the Eastern Pass. With Jones were Centurion Dane and her second adviser. Dane was decorated for his recent work in the north, and he accepted the honour graciously. Hendricks had Denzeel and Brent with him, and Gar-Tu had two young warriors on his side who had recently been promoted during the strategic training. They sat in a circle in a large tent that Hendricks had set up for this purpose. Unlike the big council in Miceen, there was no one to represent the Auxconites. This took up the first part of the discussion.

"We do not trust people who run away from a fight. We do not even know where these Auxconites come from, or what lands they inhabit!" Gar-Tu said with a brutish snarl.

"We do not know that they have betrayed us," Macy Jones reminded the leader of the hillmen. "And we do know where they live. They inhabit the outer circle of this world between the southern tip of the Great Desert and the bottom of Panwood. They have been here since the beginnings of your world, and I have confirmed this within ancient records. They are a somewhat xenophobic people and have been clear that they want no one to ever breach their borders. I will try to contact them through means that I will not explain here. So, unless anyone else has anything to say about the Auxconites, I suggest that we move on to the business of Saturn and his minions."

Quiet hung in the tent for a moment, and then Denzeel spoke up. "I was never able to truly be comfortable with Oniman. I can't really say why but I always felt that something was left unsaid; that there was another agenda. Hendricks knows that I do not fully trust the man or his people—whoever they are. We have only ever really seen a few of them."

"Be patient, my friend," Hendricks said. "If Jones, uh, the Good Goddess says that she can confirm these people and will look into the matter, then we should take her on her word. If anyone can do this, it is she." He spoke with some authority, remembering his personal glimpse into her private reality when he hung between life and death and had met the consciousness of Commander Vokova. He could only imagine how strange her existence truly was.

Denzeel nodded in compliance, and no one else spoke on the matter, so the discussion moved on to the nuts and bolts of their assembled forces and the tasks ahead of them. Hendricks, who was becoming used to having a great degree of authority, caught himself in the act of leading the talks and deferred to Jones if only because she commanded the largest of the assembled forces.

Jones, wearing a truly pained expression on her golden face, spoke of the attack and the damage done. "We have suffered a loss of three entire legions of fighters with many more wounded. A small number of the wounded will continue with us, but I have sent some back toward Miceen. Some expect to die on the road, and others to pass later with their families at their side. Any who recover will set up extra defences for the city, should we fail in our task." Turning to her companions, she said, "Centurion Dane, have you an exact number of our fighting force?"

Dane rose and drew a small scroll from a leather satchel. "We have a fighting force of 54,300. With the readmission of the training legion, we are up to 58,300. We began at nearly 70,000, so that should tell you some of the losses that we suffered."

Jones turned to Hendricks now, merely raising her unearthly eyebrows.

Hendricks rose from his seat and spoke. "The Zingaris have no city to return to or to defend, so we, in fact, have many more mouths to feed than just our fighting force. For the sake of the war, we now have 14,500 fighters. We can give another 2,000 non-combatants to assist, but I wouldn't count them in the assault force."

"And how do the Gar-Tu fare? How many do you bring against Saturn?" Jones asked the leader of the hillmen.

Gar-Tu seemed a bit off balance but then rose to emulate the form of the others. "We have 20,000 fighters," He said proudly. For whatever reason, the Gar-Tu had suffered the least number of casualties thus far.

"Then, going forward," Centurion Dane said, "We have a total of 92,800 as an invading force."

"Gentlemen," said Jones, "despite my own military training on Mars, I fear that I had acted too rashly and without caution. I hold myself responsible for the disaster of the Eastern Pass. I was overconfident that our superior numbers would overwhelm Saturn's forces. I now see the error of my ways and insist that all of you voice how you think we should proceed. My mistake has cost us dearly, and I fear that we have lost whatever advantage we had."

Brent spoke up then, surprising everyone. "You are a good leader. You have nothing to regret. The best of warriors can fall under an ambush and we will be stronger for the knowledge. I have met this Saturn, and he is evil. Sometimes evil can be very sneaky, and this is how it was. We will prevail, I'm sure."

"The monster has no honour. We will crush them surely," Gar-Tu said.

"Do not underestimate this creature!" Jones was on her feet now, and her voice rang inside the tent. "This alien thing has caused your people the misery of war for centuries; your very history is written in blood. We must be as cunning and ruthless as it is if the people are ever to be free of war. One more massive campaign of bloodshed to end all war in Terraroma!" she cried

The sudden explosion of emotion moved Hendricks. He would always remember those words. Hendricks recalled the tale of how Jones avenged the death of her lover, Prisca. She had battled the avatar of Olympias to the death, but it was really Loki; it was always only the alien, the thing they now called Saturn.

The leaders talked well into the early evening and then continued on into the night until they had a final plan of attack. They did not break for a meal or pause at all for longer than 15 minutes. Finally, when all but the details that had to wait for circumstance to dictate them had been laid out, they stopped. They had devised a plan to break the city's defences by using some of the extra power packs. If they could get through the city wall, the invasion could be quicker. If, according to the plan, they could enter the city with the laser weapons early in the siege, perhaps the war could be won quickly and save many a life.

Hendricks could still see problems with the plan. Jones argued that a gamble was worth the potential victory. It was dubbed Operation Spearhead.

Finalized though the plan might be, Hendricks knew that the debate between him and Jones had not yet reached a conclusion. He assumed that Jones knew this too.

21

GHOSTS IN THE MACHINE

JONES SIGNALLED TO the men with the horns. *Sound the stop. We will march no more today.* Within minutes, the perimeter was being secured, and camp was being set. Hendricks, with his keen eyes, had reported to her that a suitable area was available, and she knew from his tone that he would be visiting her soon; they were perhaps a week out from Necropolis, and he likely could not stay silent any longer. He had never been happy with the attack plan and had only signed off on it because she had agreed to speak with him again before they arrived. He would need to be reassured. But before that happened, she had another meeting to attend, an in-camera meeting with the other Magnus 9 matrix AI system components.

She sat atop her mount and watched the enormous army proceed past her; when the camp was in position, and the armies settled to her satisfaction, she retired to her war tent. She wrote a quick message to Hendricks for him to meet her there at 1900 hrs. She sent the message off with a herald and gave instructions to her personal guard that she was not to be disturbed except under the direst circumstances.

There was a big difference between herself, the Good Goddess, and the other two avatars that had gone before her. She had been alive when the transformation took place, whereas the other avatars—Olympias and Magnus Jupiter—were merely built from the biomatter of the dead; they were empty shells for the alien to inhabit. She, Macy Jones, was part of the mental matrix of the Magnus 9 AI; her mind itself was partially used to support the incredible logistics of running the world ship, the untapped potential of her human brain put to work. Yet, somehow, she was still herself, the same autonomous being she had always known herself to be.

She stretched her muscles slowly and came to rest in a most comfortable position among several large pillows pilled upon her bed. Jones didn't sleep anymore, not in the human sense anyway, but she did take a rest period a few times a week. She thought of it as regeneration time. That was what was happening right now.

Macy Jones, the part of her that identified as an independent force in the universe, began to float, and the world became dim and pastel, impressionist. Jones was aware, dimly, of the tent around her, but she had mostly departed.

She was in the place she thought of as the command room, and she was not alone. The presence of the Magnus 9 AI was there and felt like a heat of intellect. It appeared like a nearly faceless humanoid, a mere impression. Commander Vokova was there, and he appeared as he had been centuries ago when he uploaded his mind into the Magnus 9 matrix. His image sputtered like a drifting television reception.

"You are ignoring calls to council as you yourself suggested them. Why Jones?"

"There is no point in listening to your objections when I am already aware of them," Jones replied.

"You are acting unilaterally, Macy Jones," came the voice of the Magnus 9 system itself. It sounded like a machine, and Jones knew this was by choice; it could sound like anyone at all. It was electronic instead. Its tone was always neutral and detached. She was *inside* it. *She was part of it.* She hated thinking about it, analyzing the situation. She was a madwoman, talking to herself, an AI, and a ghost.

"Are you denying the evidence that the alien, the thing you like to call Loki, still lives here in Terraroma? Well, out here in the flesh and blood, it calls itself Saturn, and it is murder," said Jones to no one in particular.

"You are giving it exactly what it wants, war. It will become stronger as the carnage piles up," Vokova said, his expression that of a man pleading. Something about how he communicated was always exaggerated.

"To wage war is what you have always said that you wanted to stop happening in Terraroma. Yet, you yourself ride out at the head of the procession!" The Magnus 9 system merely outlined the issue. "You are right to worry about the alien, but I fear you don't understand the danger. If you are killed in battle, you will die within the matrix, and there will be fewer T-waves to hold this world together. This could mean the final demise of the *Crimson Sta*r and all who live aboard her."

"If I didn't know that you were a machine, Magnus 9," Jones replied to the intellect, "I would think that you have a cruel streak. Must you always remind me of my fate? Must you always point out that the system relies on the extra T-waves from my life force?"

"It is an inescapable fact that much damage was suffered," the Magnus 9 continued. "You have made your choice."

Jones turned her attention away from the Magnus 9 and looked at Vokova. He was leaning against nothing, merely adopting an attitude of great stress. His figure had been hunched, but now he straightened out and, to Jones' surprise, reached out and took her hand. "This place was a paradise once, and it perhaps could be again in time if we improve upon it gradually. Educate the population. Strive for improvement. We have time, Macy Jones. We have time on our side, and perhaps before long, we could create a crew for this ship and begin to effect repairs. Perhaps if you knew what this place once was." Vokova spoke with passion in his voice, and he continued to hang onto her.

Jones realized that he was trying to show her something. She felt her essence being lifted into the familiar red field, which she now realized had changed since she joined with the matrix. She was inside the vast network of the world ship's AI system, and that vastness had been represented in a field of red in the beginning. Slowly, it had become blended with a rich blue hue, and the mindscape had become purple, at times a deep purple.

She soared upward until finally she realized that she was high up in the atmosphere of Terraroma and she was sailing over the landscape from the vantage point of the sun line. Behind her was the great spine of the world, the Blue Mountains, running north to south. She was travelling due north and had passed over the Long Sea. Small settlements of modern design were visible here and there, and the surrounding landscape was much lusher than the lands she knew now. As she continued, she saw how the area she knew now as the Great Desert had once been a small ocean. Vast and blue, it bent around the curve of the world and Jones felt such a rush of emotion as she had felt in many years. This was the world of the *Crimson Star* before the disaster that had changed her forever. A modern metropolis sprawled on the northeast shore of the ocean; skyscrapers pushed up into the hazy air. This is where the badlands were now.

Vokova's message ended as quickly as it had begun. His visage stood back from her now, his arms folded.

Jones stepped forward and began to speak. She felt oddly more human than she had in a long time. "It was I who pushed the alien out before. I who sacrificed herself to save this world from sudden decay. It is cold hate and steel intellect, this creature that has stolen the body of General Marcellus. If nothing is done about Saturn, he will at the very least continue to wage war across these lands."

"You are very selfish to risk death in these wars!" Vokova exclaimed.

Then the cold voice of the Magnus 9 system stated, "The odds are against you, Jones. Your chances are at best ten to one that you can defeat Saturn without being killed or injured. If you are killed, and nothing replaces your T-waves, then the habitat of Terraroma will begin a slow, inevitable decline over the next century. Shortly thereafter, all life here will die."

Jones was exasperated. How could she make them understand the plan? "Saturn is hate, and I drove him out with love, with emotions that he actually fears. You cannot equate those things, and they are the best weapons against it. I must confront him personally, and to do that, we must drive his army back before it's too late and getting close to the thing is impossible!"

The debate became a stalemate. Jones was glad that the meeting turned to more practical matters of the running of the environment. This happened in an almost limbo state; the great cylinder was being cared for, she was recharging her avatar, and last but not least, she was off in a corner, trying to think. Time passed, and she had no concept of it for a while. Finally, the session seemed to draw to a close, and she saw the two shapes again: the AI and the ghost.

"Only you can act physically in this world, Macy Jones. The Good Goddess," said the apparition of the Russian Commander.

"That was your idea, Vokova," Jones said quietly. She waited a moment and then continued. "Back on Mars, I remember my old man telling me a secret. I was a small kid, and I was getting bullied at school. He told me that the only thing you can do with a bully is punch him in the nose. The alien, Saturn is a bully."

"Consider all of us Jones. That is what we ask," said the AI.

"There is one other thing. Details of the investigation you asked for regarding the people called the Auxconites." The AI continued. "The information is now released and is coming online. It will be in your head anytime now."

Jones was in an odd state now, in flux within the matrix but also relaxed and comfortable on her bed among the pillows. The lamps in the tent were low, so the light was subdued. She was thinking about the Auxconites and was distracted. She reached out again with her mind as only she could do; her mind travelled farther than anyone realized she could. Silently, she touched the mind of an apprentice who she kept secret and he, within a trance and safely hidden in a secret refuge, began to transcribe the new information about the Auxconites. It would be safely stored in a scroll in the hidden refuge. She had set this plan into action months ago before setting out on the warpath. The action complete, she began to return to normal consciousness in her war tent.

Then she suddenly realized that someone was in the tent with her. Shadows of brown and grey seemed to leap around the room as she picked up the nearest lamp to turn it up. A hooded figure of a man was sitting in a chair off to the left of her bed. She started quickly as a cat coming up in a defensive position.

The man dropped his hood, and it was Hendricks.

"How the hell did you get in here?" Jones exclaimed. She was on her feet now and drew her sword on instinct.

"You going to arrest me, Captain Jones?" Hendricks said, without changing his position or moving a muscle. Anger flashed across her golden features for a second, then the look dropped, and she tried to hide a smile. She remembered many years earlier when she had first met Hendricks; the two of them had barely escaped death, and she had scanned him with her military armband and discovered that he'd had a gang tattoo removed. Jones was very human at the time and had tried to arrest him. Well, that's another story and a long time ago.

"An old Zingaris trick I've picked up; the art of stealth," he said, standing now and offering his hand. "Don't be mad at your guards. Nobody but me could have gotten this far into your camp. I was only trying to make a point."

"And what would that be?" Jones said, almost laughing in spite of herself.

"That I am capable of a few surprises myself and you and I should be working together, not 'Strategizing around a unilateral goal' or whatever it was you said at the beginning of the war council," Hendricks said. He paused for a moment, the expression on his face changing as he searched for the right words to make his point. "We haven't had a lot of contact since your transformation into the Good Goddess, and to be completely honest, I wasn't sure how much of the Macy Jones I knew was in there."

Jones frowned when he said this, and he raised his hand before she could interrupt.

"But now I see that I was wrong. You are still here, the same nasty little army brat that I've always known. I'm sorry. Time and responsibility have made me see that I acted like a fool back then. I was there when the last battles with the alien happened. I understand how you want to do this. You want to get close enough to Saturn so you can engage him personally *and drive the thing out of that body.* I agree. It's the only way."

Jones was surprised; this was not what she had expected to hear. She had assumed that there would be more objections to her plan. "Okay, so you have my full attention; I wasn't expecting that. I could sense your desperation to speak to me before we began the assault. What is it that you needed to say so badly? I'm never wrong about these things."

"Well, you're not exactly right about it this time," Hendricks said flatly, trying to be as assertive as he could, to not be intimidated by this tall, golden-skinned woman who wore the features of Macy Jones. "I agree that this is probably the best way to stop Saturn, but I have no intention of being on the other side of the city with the Zingaris when you come face to face with him. Denzeel can lead in my absence. Let me come with you and help you fight your way to Saturn. How exactly do you intend to find him, anyway?"

"Leave that up to me. I'll be getting some help from my friends inside the system," Jones said and gave him an approving nod.

Hendricks gave her a big grin in return.

"There is something that I have learned from the others, something I just learned a few moments ago, that you need to hear about," Jones said.

Hendricks raised his eyebrows in question, and she continued.

"I put the task to Vokova and Magnus 9 of gathering whatever information they could regarding the Auxconites. What they found out was disturbing. These people, who are the descendants of the original survivors like everyone else on the *Crimson Star*, as you know, have been living in the outer sections of the ship. They have been exposed to radiation from space in ways that the people inside the environment never were. They are mutants; the strange illusions that they can project, I think, are the result of the exposure.

"But what is worse is that they are xenophobes and religious fanatics as well. How their beliefs work, I can't say that I completely understand, but it's all a mythologized account of their survival in the outer parts of the ship. I could find nothing out about what became of Oniman after he parted ways with Denzeel. It was suggested that if we are to encounter them again, to be cautious."

She paused for a moment and a serious expression came into her golden features. "Hendricks, these Auxconites feel that our arrival in Terraroma, in the *Crimson Star*, is some kind of important religious event."

Hendricks spoke to her in some detail of his experience in the badlands, a tale that concerned Jones even more. He told her that he had wondered later if Saturn could somehow have been responsible, perhaps trying to prevent him from reaching the power supply. Surely the thing knew the interior of the *Crimson Star* backwards and forward considering how long it had been inside the "mind" of the ship.

Jones said that she doubted it; the events seemed more like something the Auxconites would do, with their odd brand of non-violence. Not much could be done at this point about the Auxconites unless they decided to show themselves again.

It was time to prepare for Operation Spearhead.

22

WAR CRY!

THREE DAYS LATER, Hendricks was returning to the main camp after having gone ahead with scouts to assess the defence capabilities of Necropolis. He had paid careful attention to the Blue Mountains to the east, but even with his advanced vision, he could not see any sign of the glider attack force or even gauge where they were positioned in the highlands. He wondered if that tactic had run its course now that Saturn knew his enemies had laser weapons that could bring down any flyer from a good distance. Better to not rule out any possible threat; they could merely be hidden. A large forest, shown on the maps as Darkwood, made it hard to see the lower hills of the mountain range. Even with his added abilities, he couldn't see everything.

He would return to his Zingaris today and give them a speech before the major assault upon Necropolis began. He very much wanted to talk with Helen as well; she had taught him that he could still be happy, even in this crazy world. Now he could imagine a time when this was over, and they could truly relax and live without the threat of war. This wasn't going to be a happy occasion; it never was, anyway, when one set off to war. Dark clouds on the wind, both in the northlands skies and upon their hearts. Hendricks suddenly felt alive. There was thunder in his heart. He was confident that this would be the final battle and that Saturn, at least, would be destroyed.

That evening, after the day's business was done, Helen and Hendricks relaxed in their tent. Helen had decided to work as a medic, although the law said that she must be armed with at least a bayonet. She did, gladly and had another weapon as well. The Zingaris had a throwing weapon that was sort of similar to a light metal boomerang, but smaller. One would throw what look like a metal disc, and then, when it was in flight, they would whistle, and the disk would change direction quickly, surprising the target. Completely defensive.

As they reclined among great stuffed pillows and linens, Helen, without a word, leaned over and kissed Hendricks.

He responded appreciatively but with some surprise. "I thought that you were angry with me for going off with the Good Goddess."

"You mean Macy Jones," Helen said quietly, and Hendricks raised his eyebrows. She continued. "That's who she is, and I'd rather you were fighting beside her than leading the Zingaris assault. I can't really explain what it's like to be in the thing's presence—I mean, I know how you fought Magnus Jupiter, and that was the alien, but now, as Saturn, the thing's spirit is animating the corpse of General Marcellus, and that was truly horrible. He was dead, gone, and something evil was inside his rotting body. Something held it all together, but it had its failings as well. The cheeks of his face hung like curtains stretched over a skull."

"Damn," was all Hendricks could say.

"No, I don't really like you being on the other side of the battle, but what can I do? I feel like I've been caught in a high wind ever since I met you." Helen smiled as she spoke. "You're the only thing that's helped me keep it together in this odd world. I don't want tomorrow to come." She snuggled in closer to him.

He gathered her up in his arms, and he was as happy as he ever got.

Soon the only light in their tent was the glow of their bodies. When the next day was uncertain, as it always is in war, that glow burns a little brighter.

Hendricks told Brent to take his orders from Denzeel. He would be leading the Zingaris, and Brent was told to trust him implicitly; Hendricks had gone on that there was no one person in all of Terraroma that he trusted more than Denzeel. The man Denzeel, now of the Zingaris, late of Miceen, was smart, faithful, strong, and had balls of steel. Hendricks had been wandering around this great circular world with Denzeel for six years now and had said he was still alive because of being with Denzeel. A man to put your faith in.

So, he reported to Denzeel and got to hear what Hendricks had said about him now. Denzeel told him that Hendricks had said Brent was tough and smart. And honest for a smuggler, whatever that meant. The two men knew each other well enough but had never had reason to work together until now. They went over the assault plan and their places in it.

The two men sat in a large war tent, which was big enough to accommodate the full Zingaris leadership. Later, the full complement of Zingaris leaders would be present and briefed on the siege and initial assault details. The old wolves and a few others already knew the basics of what was supposed to happen; for example, they already knew that Denzeel had been appointed general and that Hendricks would be assisting the Good Goddess. The old wolves hadn't liked this one bit, but they feared displeasing the goddess; they also assumed that Hendricks was acting on the goddess's request. It was also known that if Hendrick were to fall in battle, then Denzeel was to take the position of Tyrr, at least temporarily. Before the others arrived, Denzeel went over the plan with Brent.

"We are going to attack the upper northeast wall of Necropolis," Denzeel said and produced a map that had been drawn on parchment. "We will be here," he pointed. "We'll be between many of the Miceen army. There will be three legions to the north of us trying to storm the main gates and south of us another four legions working with the siege towers whose construction will be complete by tomorrow morning."

"Not the entire compliment!" Brent said and felt a bit foolish as soon as the question came out.

"No, of course not. Those who assist and many other families will remain here at this camp for a time," Denzeel said. "One-third of our archers, the very best we have, will assist the Gar-Tu, who will be clearing a small woodland and invading a logging camp outside the southwest wall. They are to secure wood to build siege boats. We have requested as strongly as possible that they avoid killing if possible—take prisoners perhaps, but I have little faith that it will happen. The Gar-Tu have animalistic souls, I think. They smell blood; it will be a slaughter, certainly."

"I have spent much time with them," Brent said. "I found them to be very honourable. I think that they will surprise you, Denzeel. General Denzeel, I should say. Congratulation on the position. The people have great respect for you."

"Thank you." Denzeel nodded in his humble fashion. "To continue, Centurion Dane, with three legions, will attach the main gate. It is quite possible they will meet resistance on the ground there. There will be siege towers deployed to our south. Here, south of that, will be Hendricks and Jones—the goddess, I mean. They plan to try to kill the monster Saturn and with him the demon who controls him. They'll use the weapons from their world and smash their way into the city to kill him. They've told me that they'll blast a hole in the city wall. I have great faith in them, but I do not fully understand."

"I think that I have an idea what they are going to do," Brent said. "I've seen the arsenal that Hendricks brought back from the badlands. He had several charged power packs that could recharge both the laser rifle and pistol. One or two of those packs on backup might actually blow a hole in a city wall. Well, depending on the wall itself. It might just work." Brent shrugged.

"Those magic weapons are precarious, at best," Denzeel said with a snort. "They are deadly, however. More deadly than any weapon I have ever seen."

After a moment's thought, Denzeel continued. "As you've heard in councils, we believe that the enemy forces are weakened by the battle at the Eastern Pass. Let's be honest, the Miceenians got their asses kicked, but the Saturnian forces got *their asses* kicked and then handed to them. So, it makes sense that we try to press that advantage. The Gar-Tu will be attacking in the southern side of the walls with the Miceenians more in the north, and the Zingaris spread around according to the need."

Thunder rumbled in the distance, coming closer. Brent turned at the sound. "That sounds like an omen to me."

"It is not an omen; it is the will of the goddess," Denzeel replied with a grim look.

* * *

An incredible flash of lightning illuminated the landscape. Tens of thousands of soldiers marched in tight unison across the land, making the very ground rumble as they headed north. With them were cavalry, horse-drawn carts of various sizes, and siege towers that rolled upon huge wheels and loomed over the procession like vampires. Thunder crashed a second behind the flash.

Another longer flash with a simultaneous thunderclap came again. Across the plain, enemy soldiers poured out of the city gates to take up positions of defence.

The day had arrived.

Hendricks rode his mount forward toward the head of a column of the army where Jones and Centurion Dane were riding together. He noticed the expression on Dane's face change when he saw how Hendricks had changed his attire. He looked less the desert warrior and more Miceenian Commander than any other time Dane had seen him. Gone was the loose desert garb, now replaced with sensible armour—a leather chest plate, protective shin guards, and brass wrist supports. A strong Miceenian helmet, this one with a black horsehair plume, sat on his head. Finally, he wore a blood-red cloak, as symbolic to the Miceenians as it had been to the Romans those thousands of years ago back on Earth. A leather strap with Zingaris decor held the laser rifle over his left shoulder.

"Nice weather for a battle," Hendricks said as he came up beside Jones.

"I have ordered up the nastiest gloom I could. Vokova has stopped arguing with me now. He knows that we won't stop, so he is helping out by temporarily tweaking the environmental settings," Jones said, her golden features as unreadable as ever. "I'm sure that Saturn can appreciate it. I just want the best cover we can get so our explosives can be set up."

"All right. We have to deal with this first." Hendricks gestured toward the city they approached. He had been here before. The city had been called Augustine then, and many of the soldiers in the Miceenian force had been here six years ago when the avatar Magnus Jupiter was brought down.

"No worries. We shall deal with this, but we stay back until the plains before the city are secure. Do not join the battle. We will plant our bomb during the chaos, but we wait till the way is won," Jones said, her flat tone bordering on sounding like a command.

Hendricks merely nodded his consent. He knew that he had more practical battlefield experience than Jones but that she had military training with the Sol System Peacekeepers. He was deferring to her because the plan to stop Saturn was a good one. He almost laughed aloud as he realized that here, moments before the start of battle, he was dreaming of peace. Peace in a land that had known only war.

Thunder crashed and great brass horns blasted the wet air. The procession picked up its pace, and as it did so, Centurion Dane rode over beside Hendricks.

"Success, John Hendricks. Success or die well," Dane said to him. "Send this demon back to hell! Good luck. I ride to assault the main gate. I ride with three legions now." Dane held out his arm, and Hendricks grabbed it with his own. The two men shook hands for a moment, and then Dane saluted him in a comic manner. Hendricks smiled and watched the man ride off.

Jones called a halt. She rode her mount up onto a low hill overlooking the city. She had never seen Necropolis—or Augustine, as it had once been called—in person before; she had seen the place in the matrix, more as a vision than anything. A tall, dark tower rose out of centre of the city like a drawn sword held up high in defiance. They had reached the place where they would attack. Already, to the south, cavalry rode down onto the plain to meet the men who would defend the city. He had always led the Zingaris into battle, and he felt bad, sitting here on his mount, watching men ride to their deaths.

Messengers were sent running with new orders. Jones was directing the attack with the intention of clearing a path for Hendricks and her to plant the bomb. With her, 100 of the best fighters in nine legions. They would come with Jones and Hendricks when they entered the city. For one agonizing hour, Hendricks stood beside Jones and watched the battle play out on the plains before the east side of the city. So far, she had every reason to believe that the enemy was at a disadvantage as she watched her army do its gruesome work. They clearly had the advantage on the plain, and soon the defending army was split into two groups, both now fighting to stay alive.

Overhead, the dark clouds crashed again and again, sending lightning cracking through the atmosphere. No one alive in the cylinder had ever seen storms like these. It was all mostly gloom with lightning and no rain. Thunder came and went, and it was all so violent at times it was frightening.

Finally, Jones gave the signal, and they began to ride down to the wall of the city. Hendrick rode up beside Jones, and together they led the way to their destination. One hundred of Miceen's best warriors galloped beside and ahead of them, spears poised to strike. Soon they were in the midst of the battle and riding hard toward their destination. The specially picked warriors did their work savagely and efficiently, and Hendricks felt a surge of optimism in spite of the carnage that was spread around them.

In a flash of lightning, Hendricks saw that they were maybe 100 yards from the city wall. It was difficult to judge exactly where on the city wall they were, but Jones pulled ahead confidently, and Hendricks trusted that Jones knew they were in position. Now to set the charge. On either side, the Miceenian warriors held back the defending soldiers with shields and spears.

Jones signalled to two men behind them, who came forward with a makeshift ladder. They were up close to the wall now, and the ladder was pushed up against the city fortifications; it reached perhaps 20 yards up the city wall. Jones dismounted, reached into a saddlebag, and produced two of the backup power packs. Then she reached deeper into the bag and brought out a handful of dark grey putty.

Hendricks looked up to the top of the city wall above where they were; archers scurried into place and drew back their bows as they took aim at Jones. Quickly, he swung the laser rifle around and fired at the men high above. Green fire shot out like lightning, and three of the archers were obliterated in a heartbeat. Some others broke and ran from their place on the wall while at least two more held their places and sent arrows whistling down at Jones.

Jones had already begun to climb the ladder, and she had her military armband deployed. The arrows bounced harmlessly off her invisible shield as she continued to climb. Soon she reached the position she wanted, and she pushed the power packs and the putty hard against the brick of the wall. Below, Hendricks continued to fire at the defenders high above. Finally, with the packs in place and secured, Jones stepped off the rungs of the ladder and came sliding down the ladder at a generous speed. She let out a wild war cry that Hendricks had never heard the likes of before.

This is what we have come to, he thought darkly as Jones's war cry echoed in his thoughts. *We are truly one of the inhabitants now.*

Jones quickly remounted her horse and moved back away from the wall.

Hendricks followed quickly behind her; now, it was time for him to do his part in this stage of the operation. He directed his mount around in a tight circle and brought the horse to rest in the place he wanted. He dismounted and swung the laser rifle around in front of him once again. He looked back over his shoulder at Jones, who was watching a short distance behind him. She nodded grimly to him, and he made a quick adjustment to the weapon in his hands. Now he knelt with the rifle and took careful aim at the power packs that Jones had adhered to the city walls.

Jones called out an order for the elite force to get ready.

Hendricks fired the weapon, and at first, nothing seemed to happen. He could almost feel the uncertainty in the soldiers around him. Surely they noticed the tracer line shooting out to the target on the walls. Thunder rumbled overhead, and this time, a great muffled rumble began to run through the very ground. Moments later, the power packs whined, and a massive explosion blasted brick and mortar in all directions.

A large section of the wall that fortified Necropolis fell away in a cloud of dust and debris. Bodies fell with the debris, and cries were heard mixed within the great crashing of the section of wall coming down. Chunks of brick flew outward, and many of the Miceenian soldiers knelt with their shields over their heads to protect themselves. A massive cloud of dust rose from the still falling rubble, obscuring the true damage that the blast had done.

Cries and curses from the dust came, and slowly the wind blew it away to reveal a huge section of the wall had fallen from top to bottom. A large passageway into Necropolis had been created. They looked into the city directly toward the palace of Saturn.

The Miceenian force let out a roar.

Jones drew her sword and lifted it high. "Forward!" she cried.

***

Saturn looked down from high above in the great tower section of his new palace. He watched as the eastern wall was breached by a massive explosion. A sudden involuntary shudder ran through him, and he knew that it did not originate in *his* soul. The thing that was alien realized that the host body he had taken possession of was not dead; the soul that was Marcellus was still alive. A very complicated moment of self-actualization was happening; what was he? An entity from the wastes of space that knew not if it was unique but one of others who lived in this alternate dimension of time-space. A thing that loved pain and suffering, anguish with a little fear on top. Was it Marcellus? Born and raised in Miceen as proud and ambitious as any military leader before him.

No. The Saturn thing squashed the Marcellus part like a cigarette under a boot. Yet an ember still burnt.

It was itself again! It was Saturn, the sole ruler and demi-god of the people of Necropolis. Warlord and soon to be sole ruler of all Terraroma.

She was coming at last. The Macy Jones creature Saturn hated more than any others, for it was she who had ousted him from his nest in the matrix of the ship's AI system. She who threw out emotions of the opposite kind, which the alien feared so. She who turned off fear and filled her being with images that were repulsive to his being.

He looked down and saw Simon with a cohort of soldiers, moving toward the east wall where the invaders were entering the city. *At last, she has come.* Saturn grinned through the ruined face of General Marcellus. He had always known that Jones would attempt to confront him directly; she would try to finish the job she started years ago. She had pushed it out and taken its position within the matrix and, in the following years, tried to teach the Miceenians a new way to live, a way of peace. Meanwhile, he had done just the opposite with the people of this city; he had rewarded the cruel and savage among the citizens. Conquest and war were their future, and it would be until this entire habitat was under his boot. He continued to watch as Simon moved down the main eastern avenue.

23

FOLLY AND FATE

CENTURION DANE SHOUTED orders from his mount. The great battering ram, the grandfather of the one used in the Augustine conquest, was called up and positioned to assault the city's main gate. The ram itself was a gift from the Gar-Tu, a symbol of friendship and mutual respect after the Miceenians had taken the time to parlay with the hillmen and eventually share military knowledge with them. Now the ram was in position, and dozens of soldiers began to swing the ram to build momentum. Dane climbed up the outside of a nearby siege machine and raised his sword high in one hand while holding onto the war tower with the other.

"Strike!" he hollered to the soldiers below, and the first blow against the city's main gates was struck. Everything shook with the terrible impact of the ram.

Boom! but the gates held. *Boom!* Again, and the earth shook, and the gates held. Over and over, the ram struck, and now Centurion Dane looked to the back end of the ram to make sure that a fresh crew was ready to take over when the first one grew weary. The thunder of the ram's assault became a steady, consistent rumble. Overhead, the sky flashed as the rainless storm continued and then fell back to the low, gloomy ceiling of clouds.

An hour into the initial assault, the sudden sound of an explosion on the east wall tore through the battle atmosphere, and Dane used that moment to change crews on the battering ram. He knew the explosion was coming, and upon hearing it, he filled with optimism and the wild passions of battle. This was the life that Centurion Dane knew best, and all he had done and trained for was focused on this moment. Victory!

"Put your backs into it, you dogs!" he shouted down to the new crew on the ram.

Suddenly, a sharp crack rang out in the air. Dane twisted around at the noise; it was a strange and unfamiliar noise to him. *Crack!* Again, and this time, a soldier higher above him on the tower clutched at himself and fell headlong from the structure. *Crack! Crack!* and two more soldiers dropped like flies. Dane had no idea what was going on, and he scanned the area around him. What new devilry was this? Then he saw men up on the city walls with weapons that looked similar to the mad fire stick Hendricks had brought into the battle at the Eastern Pass; five of them were leaning over the wall and pointing the long barrels at easy targets, but no green fire leaped out as it had with Hendricks's weapon. *Crack!* Dane pulled himself along the side of the tower, so he was on the backside of the siege machine and had some cover.

Many more defending soldiers appeared on high city walls, but these were archers and they let loose a deadly volley of arrows.

"Take cover!" Centurion Dane screamed at the soldiers on the battering ram. They immediately dropped the battering ram and pulled their shields out over their heads to protect themselves from incoming arrows. Dane realized quickly that the archers were aiming at everything they could except the battering ram. The defenders with the new weapons came along the wall until they were above the gates and began firing projectiles at the assault on the gate. At first, the soldiers on the battering ram seemed safe beneath the canopy of shields, but then, after multiple hits, the shields began to break, and large pieces blew right off. Finally, a soldier was hit, and as he fell, the group on the battering ram broke formation and fled the position in a panic. Many were cut down by archers as they ran.

"Damn you, fools!" Centurion Dane cried in despair. "Fall back. Fall back and regroup on the plain!"

* * *

Denzeel and the Zingaris, the main contingent with Brent in attendance, rode out toward the enemy forces that came around from the south of the city. Unlike the rest of the assembled desert warriors, Brent hadn't been born into one of the twelve houses that made up the basis of Zingaris society. So, he'd had to pledge allegiance to one of them, and he chose the current ruling house, the sign of the lion. This was Hendricks's house and Helen's as well. It made sense for Brent to do that, but he heard the remarks from the population. *Another outsider joins the House of the Lion. The* wolves *say one must bleed in battle to join a house.* These were the sort of things Brent would hear whispered too loudly behind his back.

Fuck them, he thought as he and the other riders began to speed up to a gallop. *Blood is cheap in this madhouse, and I'll likely be bleeding before this is over.* They were racing straight toward the Necropoline line, and Denzeel, his weapon held high, was leading the charge

"Death to Saturn!" Denzeel bellowed out, and then in the next moment, it happened. The defending line, instead of charging forward, knelt in formation and stayed their ground. Every fifth man did not have a shield but was instead aiming a weapon similar to the laser rifle which he himself had used in the past. *We are doomed!* he thought in horror, thinking that the enemy had many laser rifles.

The new weapons gave off a backfire kick, and several incoming Zingaris riders fell, their horses as well, sometimes hit, other times tripping over fallen mounts. The next line of horsemen tried to stop suddenly, but many failed and went down as well. Denzeel cursed through his astonishment.

"Guns!" cried Brent. "These sons of bitches have guns! Denzeel, tell the men to fall back before they're slaughtered." Brent was stunned by what he was seeing, but he began to understand what had happened. *This has to be Simon's doing. Just like the flyers, he's developing better weapons. He has taught them how to make flintlocks, probably the easiest thing given what resources were available.*

Brent struggled to control the mounting fear in his gut, and he looked at the new weapons as closely as he could. Yes, they had firearms, some type of rifle with a long barrel and one hell of a kick. From what he knew of ancient weapons, a flintlock was a good guess.

He suddenly had a very bad feeling, a knot in his gut that he didn't want to acknowledge, yet it was always there, like a truth that couldn't be erased. In any struggle of force, the side with the superior technology usually won. Is that why he'd been so confident that his side would win the day? Jones and Hendricks had laser weapons, and that almost made them invincible. Wasn't that what he had tucked away in the back of his mind? Hendricks had warned him about being overconfident about the tech weapons; Brent and Simon had been armed with lasers when they arrived, but it didn't take much to turn the tables on them, did it? Damn the whole thing.

Another explosion, just to the south, shattered the air and Brent swung his head around to see what was happening. One of the siege towers had been blown up, and he had turned just in time to see the flaming structure topple to one side and crash to the ground. Burning soldiers fell or leaped from the tower as it fell. Simon had found another application for gunpowder, damn his dark soul. A helpless fury grabbed hold of Brent, and he silently wished he'd have the chance to see Simon again. And kill him.

Brent bent low on his horse as he turned to continue his retreat. The Zingaris were in a full, panicked departure from whatever the range of those new weapons was. Many had dismounted and were trying to run with their horses to present less of a target. They were unorganized, and now Necropolis soldiers were charging after them with swords and spears. Blood was spilling now, and many Zingaris turned to fight. The battle was met, but the desert warriors found themselves on the defensive; Saturn's soldiers were winning the day on this battlefield.

Brent saw Denzeel then. He was riding high on his mount and organizing the Zingaris as best he could. They needed to fall back and reorganize before Saturn's men pressed their advantage as hard as they could. Finally, through sweat and blood, Denzeel managed to organize a line of men who fought well together. Denzeel was bringing his horse around to ride to the other end of the line when a soldier burst out from a knot of Saturn's people and charged straight at Denzeel. The man leaped as high as he could, and grabbed hold of Denzeel's waist and saddle.

Denzeel's mount reared up as the two men struggled. Denzeel shifted his sword around to dispatch this madman. Seconds before Denzeel swung the blade down, the soldier hung on with one arm and stabbed down into Denzeel's leg. He howled in pain even as his blade came down and split the soldier's face in two. The soldier let out a garbled scream and fell to the ground.

Denzeel straightened up in his saddle and, holding the reins and his sword in one hand, he pressed the other against the stab wound in his leg. It was small but deep and bleeding badly. He turned to go when he heard the loud crack of the gun and felt pressure in his chest. He didn't feel pain. Another shot, and he felt like he'd been punched in the gut. Now pain radiated through his torso.

Denzeel didn't even feel the third shot. He'd been hit square in the side of his head. He fell from the mount into a heap on the ground. Dead.

Brent was gripped with emotion as he witnessed Denzeel's death. Everything around him seemed to slip into slow motion, and he felt oddly as if he was watching himself act from another place. He leaped backwards and rolled behind the fallen bodies of two horsemen and their mounts. *Crack, crack, crack!* Bullets slammed into the dead flesh of the fallen as Brent came up out of the roll unharmed with sword drawn.

Hatred burnt in him and overcame common sense; he threw himself forward toward the front line of Saturn's soldiers. There were five men: three with flintlock guns and two with swords and shields trying to protect the three as they reloaded their primitive firearms. Brent swung his blade with both hands like lightning and caught the first soldier between helmet and shoulder. The man fell back with blood pumping from his severed neck; he stumbled into the second man, and blood flew into the man's eyes, blinding him. Another savage swing, and the second man fell.

One of the soldiers was reloaded, and he stood up and took aim at Brent. The other two soldiers still knelt, struggling to pack gunpowder into their new weapons. Brent swung his sword up and knocked the gun barrel away just as the flintlock fired. The bullet went nowhere, and the small explosion hit the man in his eyes. He screamed as he fell backwards, tripping over the other two. Brent came forward, gliding as if in a dream, and kicked a man in the face. The sword came up, and the sword came down again and again until Brent stood panting over five dead men.

Then everything returned to normal perception, suddenly speeding up. Brent, without another moment's thought, turned and ran.

The Zingaris contingent was in full retreat.

* * *

A couple of kilometres back from the fighting, Helen was receiving the first group of wounded as they made it back to the base for medical attention. She was helping to triage the incoming, and she could hear the distant sound of explosions. She now counted four explosions in total, and that was concerning since she had only expected to hear one. The one that Jones and Hendricks had planned to set off.

Helen had always had a strong intuition, and she had a bad feeling right now. She tried to rationalize the extra explosions, but it wasn't working well. This was a Bronze Age world, so what exactly was going bang out there?

She pushed the thoughts away and knelt before a wounded soldier, a woman in her early twenties. The offending wound was a hole in the left thigh that bled heavily. She expected a sword wound or an arrow strike. She put pressure on the wound. "Did you pull an arrow out of your thigh?"

Through gritted teeth, the woman said, "I know better."

Suddenly, the dime dropped, and she realized what she had was looking at. This was a gunshot wound! Helen rooted around the primitive equipment until she found something that would help. She was doing triage, but there was no point in passing this one on; no one here had ever removed a bullet from a wound before. She quickly worked on the bullet and then called the other medics around and explained about the new weapons and the bullets.

There would be more gunshot victims coming in.

* * *

The passage into Necropolis was hard going, not because a show of force had appeared on the other side of the broken city wall, but because a small mountain of rubble and bodies blocked the otherwise open passage. Soldiers, maybe two dozen of them, began to haul chunks of the broken wall and crushed bodies alike out of the way. This task was taking up precious time, and it wouldn't be long before Saturn's soldiers came charging in defence of the city.

"Wait!" Hendricks shouted over to Jones, and she signalled for the forces to hold up before trying to enter the city. He quickly adjusted settings on his laser rifle and began to fire at the pile of rubble before the breach in the city wall. Some debris began to glow and disappeared while some was merely blown out of the way by the force of the rifle fire. Soon he nodded over to Jones, and she gave the advance.

They were entering the city through the breach, Jones and Hendricks close to the front and among the first to get inside. Suddenly, Saturnian forces hiding near the wall began to fire their primitive guns directly at soldiers coming through the breach. Others came rushing in with swords and shields to close the breach in the wall. Now, unexpectedly, Hendricks, Jones and maybe fifty of her fighting force were completely cut off from the other legions.

Jones rode her mount over to the centre of their group and called the forces into formation. They quickly formed a circle around the Good Goddess and her helper, the Tyrr of the Zingaris. Jones signalled to a centurion the direction she wanted to move her forces in; west, toward the palace tower. The tower itself was a creepy copy of the palace tower in Miceen where she, herself, lived. When the city of Miceen had been founded long ago, it was modelled close to the city that its founders were exiled from, Augustine.

From 100 yards down a westward avenue came the elite of Necropolis, with Simon riding high in a chariot behind many cohorts of soldiers, shield to shield in tight formation, spears at the ready. She had never seen this Simon before, and wasn't he a sight. Tall in his chariot, he was dressed in black and red with a shining silver chest plate. His helm was black with a blood-red plume down the centre. Worst of all was his new mutant hand, insanely large, with sharp black nails. Jones ordered the soldiers into formation instantly. She drew her laser pistol.

Behind her, Hendricks grunted. "Damn straight!" He brought the laser rifle around to bear on the soldiers with the primitive guns. He fired without mercy, and some were instantly killed. Others ran off either in flames or in terror. Hendricks moved on his mount to come toward the breach in the wall; he wanted to open the way for the legions to enter the city.

Then Hendricks noticed something unusual; directly in front of him, one of his soldiers was standing casually, unarmed and smiling at him. He could not understand where the man came from because he had been firing the laser rifle in that direction. The man continued to smile and spread his arms as if in a gesture of welcome. It was an unnerving sight, this passive soldier posing casually while hell and war raged around him. Something made Hendricks dismount and walk toward the man, if only to smack him out of his stupor and get him back into the battle.

All around Hendricks, the battle was heating up; Jones was using her laser, but the Miceenians were badly outnumbered.

He moved toward the smiling soldier. Suddenly, he realized that he wasn't getting any closer to the man for all his effort. He felt dizzy, and the ground beneath his feet seemed to slip backwards away from him. He could hear the battle over his shoulder, but as soon as he focused on it, the sound faded away until it was gone, and silence filled the air. He swung around savagely, expecting to see Jones and the Miceenians battling Saturn's army. They were gone.

Where the west avenue and the battle should have been, there was now a wall. Stone and mortar, brick over brick. The wall reached higher than was possible until it disappeared in the low ceiling of cloud. Hendricks stood there, staring at the wall, irritated by the ugly silence that reigned over his senses. This had to be the Auxconites! There was no other explanation. Had they betrayed them and joined Saturn?

Hendricks shook his head like a dog shaking off water; he concentrated as hard as he could, trying break the illusions that confronted him. He turned back around to look at the silent soldier he had seen. The soldier was gone but now standing in his place, perhaps the true intruder, was

Oniman. He stood in the same posture that the soldier had been in, and Hendricks realized it had always been Oniman standing there.

"Damn you!" Hendricks yelled at him. "I'm needed in the battle. Damn your illusions."

Oniman simply stood there now, looking grim and serious.

Hendricks turned back to the wall and raised the laser rifle as to use the butt of the gun to strike with. "That wasn't there!" he cried and lunged forward as to smash the wall with his gun.

He went straight through the wall. This did not break the illusion as it had before. This time, Hendricks went tumbling into a vast white nothing. Suddenly, he was nowhere.

Silently, a hand reached around and put a cloth over his mouth and nose.

Hendricks felt his mind slipping away from him and a half-formed curse died on his lips. Blackness.

For Hendricks, the battle of Necropolis was over.

* * *

Jones was busy with the war; she fired her pistol at the most strategic targets she could find, usually anyone with one of those primitive guns that they had. Turned out the lost passenger from Brent's ship had been raising hell by changing the balance of power between the city states. *Didn't Brent say Simon had been an engineer?* She wondered what other surprises were coming.

She looked over at that moment and saw Hendricks dismount and move toward the back wall. She watched him lurching around and knew something was wrong with him; suddenly, he turned and ran straight ahead with his laser rifle raised to smash something with the butt of the weapon.

Then he simply disappeared into thin air.

Gone.

Jones was staring in disbelief. *What the hell just happened?* Her matrix connected mind searched for something in the history or logs. Some other explanation of phenomena like this. There was nothing.

Then, being completely Jones, she dismounted and ran toward the last place that Hendricks had been. She stood there, a golden avatar, scanning the area for something that made sense. Nothing. What was this? People don't just disappear into thin air.

Suddenly, there was a break in the line of her fighters. Simon was coming straight toward her in his chariot; his oversized hand grasped the front of the vehicle, and the other held some type of metal whip. She was in trouble now, and she knew it. She turned toward the oncoming assault and fired her laser pistol.

She missed. She'd fired high, trying to hit Simon, but being cautious about killing the horses that pulled his chariot. That had been a mistake.

Simon was upon her before she could re-aim the pistol. As he passed, he reached out and grabbed her head with his oversized hand. He leaped from the chariot as he did, knocking Jones off balance. His hand was so large that it gripped her entire head, completely covering her face.

Jones struggled madly. Using her extra strength from the military armband, she fought against his hand, bashing at it at times.

Simon hung on tight. With his other hand, he now swung the metal whip, and it crackled with an electronic force. The whip slapped against Jones golden-hued avatar body and hung onto her.

"How do you like that, you fucking bitch?" Jones heard Simon say. As it clung to her, the whip gave off a sharp electric charge. Her armband went dead. Then she felt something happening to her mind. Her connection to the matrix was cut off or blocked was more likely. Simon had designed this whip, which worked like a tech dampener and taser all in one.

She began to lose consciousness, and as she faded into blackness, she could hear Simon laughing to himself.

Then the universe went dark.

24

THE FALLING DARKNESS

THE ASSAULT UPON Necropolis had gone badly. Although it had begun with great optimism, careful planning, and nerves of steel, it had eventually failed. The battle had lasted perhaps four hours, and the failure was attributed to several factors. The introduction of the new weapons, the early-style guns, and the fact that three people in leadership roles had been taken out halfway through the battle were the main points. Eventually, Centurion Dane had taken control of the entire force. The introduction of the guns had decimated the Gar-Tu contingent on the far side of the city. Saturn's people must have been producing them for months.

By the time he realized failure was imminent, Dane had already given the order to retreat. While that objective was underway, another event took place; the sky, which had been under heavy cloud cover, changed dramatically. It was mid-afternoon at this time, and warm yellow sunlight poured into the gruesome scenes. Then the sun line itself changed. The warm, yellow light dimmed and became a much duller, blue-green colour. No one in the history of Terraroma had ever seen the like of this. A dimmer, dull day ruled over the land now, and the night came on swiftly; a thick, dark velvet curtain of blackness with little or to illumination from the sky.

When Jones regained consciousness, she immediately knew she was still blocked from the matrix. She felt weak and she couldn't move, but she could see well enough. She soon realized that she was strapped down on a stone dais. Beside her stood Saturn, a large, powerful creature who was almost normal in appearance, still resembling General Marcellus, whose body it actually was.

Behind him was the familiar biobed, the one that had probably been used by Magnus Jupiter. Farther back again was a strange contraption that was mostly covered with large sheets. It was shaped like a large cage, tall and thin, 25 feet by 5 feet. Tubes and lines ran along the floor and up under the sheets.

Saturn leaned over her. "Don't even think about trying to pull any of that shit you used in the matrix last time. You won't get the chance; we'll make sure that you are dead!" When she cringed, he leaned closer and inhaled. "Ah, fear. I know it well." Saturn moved away, and she saw him climbing into the biobed.

Simon appeared now. He held his oversized hand over his mouth in a gesture of mock astonishment. Then he walked over to her and quickly stabbed her with something sharp that was attached to a long electrical apparatus by some kind of cable.

Jones winced with the pain but refused to cry out.

"Brave to the end, huh?" Simon said and began to punch buttons on a control panel that she couldn't see. But she heard the sounds. "Too bad you won't be around at the end to see it. I'm making a god!" He came closer again and this time raised a huge stone hammer high up with his powerful hand.

Jones felt an electrical current running through her. Then Simon brought the hammer down. Again and again.

Soon, the Good Goddess of Miceen was dead.

***

In the great tower that loomed over Necropolis, mad light and sharp strikes of lightning flashed again and again. Below, the citizenry who looked on cringed and shrank away from the display. Even these people, corrupted and mean, felt fear while watching the unnatural light show going on above their city. The wiser folk among them perhaps contemplated the idea that they had backed the wrong man in this endless cycle of war; Saturn was an even darker deity than Magnus Jupiter had been. They had, as a people, perhaps travelled near the tower, but never had they seen the evil light show that danced in the air. They could only imagine what was happening up there on that night.

When the transformation happened, a thin figure, hidden by a fallen sheet from the giant cage, slowly dragged itself into the corner. The figure rested there and watched as the monster was brought into the world. As the alien spirit abandoned Marcellus's body, the true occupant slowly floated to the surface and reclaimed the body. Marcellus's mind, re-emerging into the world once again, was running on autopilot. Survival instinct ran the show.

He lay in the shadows and watched as the thing ripped its way out of its metal casket. It climbed out then, long lanky limbs swinging slightly as it straightened out. It was Saturn, it was the alien, it was 20-plus feet tall and looked like a nightmare on stilts. Marcellus had no reference in his culture that could identify what this being was.

Simon, who stood close by on the floor, certainly did; he knew exactly what he was looking at. This was the god Saturn as he was envisioned by the medieval painter Goya. Giant, grotesque with long black hair hanging to his shoulders. Large, bulging white eyes and a lipless maw for a mouth with jagged teeth for eating his children. This was another piece of human history that the alien had usurped from the mind of Vokova centuries ago when the entity had first formed its corporeal designs.

The two soldiers standing guard at the doorway to the circular stone chamber nearly bolted in terror when the thing emerged in his latest version of Saturn. Simon barked at them, and they stayed where they were.

"Kneel before your god," Simon ordered.

The soldiers complied. They fell to their knees in terror as the new Saturn towered over them. The giant god seemed to shiver in bliss as it felt the fear rising from the two horrified soldiers. They simply could not contain their horror.

Suddenly, it was the new god Saturn who couldn't contain itself; it reached out and grabbed one of the soldiers in its giant hand and lifted him into the air. It held him in one hand, opened its enormous mouth, and bit the man in half. As it chewed its first meal, it threw the bottom half of the man into the corner, where it landed with a wet thump.

Simon laughed as he watched the scene play out.

The other soldier ran screaming out the door, Simon's mad laughter trailing after him.

Marcellus crawled out the service entrance and was gone. Relief folded through him in spite of the pain that racked his beaten body. He was free! He was free of the thing that had stolen his body for so long. Memories of the horrors he had witnessed while being trapped inside of his usurped body, helpless to do anything but relive what this demon, who called himself Saturn now, had done while in possession of his flesh flooded his mind. Scenes of unspeakable cruelty and violence tortured him and he struggled to push them out of his head.

He was dying now, and quickly. He crawled into the shadows of the hallway and relaxed against the wall. *I am free again, at last,* he thought. A small smile formed on his ravaged face. Peace was coming. Blessed, dark peace.

Soon, Marcellus of Miceen was dead.

* * *

Brent made it back to the Zingaris camp and immediately started to look for Helen. There were many soldiers of the different armies, wounded and resting or waiting for attention. He was shaken but not wounded in any serious way. A slash across the back of his left arm had been a very close call. He noticed there were fewer Gar-Tu receiving medical help; he'd heard a hasty report that they had fared quite badly on the far side of the city and had nearly been wiped out. Nothing would surprise him now.

The hardest thing had been seeing Denzeel perish; he had grown quite fond of the man. Denzeel was the type who had many good friends, and the people would be devastated. They had lost both their Tyrr and his chosen successor.

Brent tried to clear his mind, but his thoughts were running rampant. *What had become of Hendricks?* No one seemed to know, but it was obvious that he hadn't made it out of the city. He could only assume that Hendricks was dead, although there was nothing to prove this, no eye witnesses.

The goddess, Jones, on the other hand, was a different story. Many soldiers had witnessed the creature with the giant hand take her down and drag her away. She was also presumed dead. Stranger yet was the creature that had been Simon; the bastard had been responsible for so much death.

And then there were the environmental changes that came about shortly after Jones was captured. Brent had been told about how Jones was connected to the *Crimson Star's* AI systems and how her connection to it was important for the smooth running of the world ship. He had also been told details about the alien, how it thrived on people's fear and pain and terror. The human race's first contact with an alien species and it turned out to be with this malevolent thing!

Dane ordered a further retreat before long as it was feared that Saturn would attempt to chase after them. There had been far too much loss for one day.

Brent found Helen arguing with the old wolves; she was asking for a group of warriors to attempt some type of recon mission to find out what had become of Hendricks. They would have none of it; Hendricks had fallen in battle, as far as they were concerned, and they would risk no more lives today. When Helen saw Brent approaching, she jumped up, full of hope for an instant until she saw his face; there was no reprieve from her grief to be found with him. He agreed with the old wolves; it was suicide to ride back there toward Necropolis. When he was more certain that she had exhausted her pain for the moment, he pulled her aside to speak to her privately.

"I think that we are in some big trouble here," Brent said

"Brent, you can really say some stupid things. Of course, we're in trouble. We've been in trouble since we ran from the peacekeepers way back on the ship. We can't just run away from here!" Helen said angrily.

"We can't stay here. You know that, Helen—don't think Saturn won't send troops out here." Brent spoke to her as sternly as he dared.

She stared at him hard. "The only reason we got out of Necropolis was because of Hendricks—he came in and got us out of hell, and I'm not doing any less." There were tears in her eyes, and she suddenly didn't care who saw them. The only good thing that had come out of being stuck in this mad world was John Hendricks. Now he was gone.

She couldn't accept that, wouldn't accept that.

"Helen, I think I know what's going on, and I'm sorry, but I believe Hendricks is gone. Listen to me," he pleaded. "I think the alien is back inside the matrix, inside the AI system. Some of the last men to get out of Necropolis said that they saw a monster, a giant, stepping out of the top of a tower in the city. Look at what's happening to the sun, to the weather—it's the thing forcing his will onto the system. And the thing the soldiers saw? Another avatar? I'm not going to stick around to see this thing up close!"

Brent waited long minutes before finally saying, "I'm going to find my ship and get the hell out here."

Silence, as sharp as a blade, hung between them. There was no persuading her; once her mind was made up about something, she was resolute. Well, Brent had his mind made up also.

Outside the Zingaris camp, the light was passing and darkness was falling.

Epilogue

WHATEVER DRUG IT was that was used to knock him out left Hendricks feeling hungover and disoriented. His weapons and battle gear were gone, and he was dressed in simple white cotton pants and shirt. After he came around, it took him some time to figure out what had happened to him, but it eventually became clear: he had been taken prisoner by Oniman and the Auxconites.

He was in a cell made of very strong plexiglass on the one side and bulkheads on the others. There was a sink and a toilet in one corner and a cot to sleep on but little else. No windows, just a very small vent overhead circulated air. The outline of a door was on one bulkhead and a drawer that could be used to pass food through to him.

Hendricks did not see his captors for perhaps / hours after he regained consciousness. He beat on the glass and cursed and hollered but got no reaction. Finally, after he had given up, two men and one woman entered the room through a doorway on the other side of the glass. They didn't speak at first, merely standing still and looking at him. He immediately recognized one of them.

"Oniman, you traitorous son of a bitch. What did Saturn do to make you betray us like this?" Hendricks yelled although he didn't know if they could hear him or not.

Apparently they could but not in the way that he had expected; Oniman addressed him, but Hendricks didn't see his lips move. He heard the words inside of his head.

- **We realize that you do not understand the significance of why you are here. It is God's will that you have come to be among us. It is unfortunate about the Good Goddess's passing, but it was inevitable** because she was not truly divine; this truth we always knew. She played a role in God's plan just as you do. That is all. -

Hendricks was coming to grips with this information—Jones was dead? Before he could interject, the woman of the group spoke her words inside his head just as Oniman had.

- No. She was not. - *Just a nod of her head.* - **We shall keep you safe with us until the prophecies are fulfilled at last—and then you shall pass unto glory as shall we all. ..** -

Then all three voices echoed in his head. -. **by God's will unto the end of the world!** -

"You're all a bunch of psychos," Hendricks muttered under his breath and then raised his voice angrily. "Don't you realize what we were telling you? That thing, Loki, Saturn is an alien and it's evil. It feeds on pain and fear! What happened back there?"

Oniman again. - **Your attempt to take the city failed. Your armies have been smashed. But do not despair, Mr. Hendricks. It has been foretold, and it is God's will. ..** -

The chorus again. -. .. **unto the end of the world.** -

Hendricks turned away from his strange captors as he felt a scream trying to rise in his throat.

He could still hear them in his head.

- **We are the righteous. You are the catalyst. All is the will of God.** -
- **Unto the end of the world.** -

This time Hendricks did scream, letting himself fall back against one of the bulkheads. He thought of Jones, and Helen and Denzeel and Brent, and he wept quietly with despair.

THE END

To be continued in Dark Star.

Printed in Canada